Here's what critics are saying about the Danger Cove Mysteries:

"High-octane entertainment and doesn't dip into a lull for even a sec! 5 stars!"
~ *Long Island Book Review*

"I am a frequent visitor to Danger Cove, and eager to stay for a long time. The mystery is very clever... put your inner Sherlock into high gear! Mixing it with some personal peril leads readers to a great conclusion…Loved it!"
~ *Kings River Life Magazine*

"The Danger Cove series continues to entertain as it showcases the talent of the GHP writers. This book is a keeper...I highly recommend this book!"
~ *Authors on the Air*

"One funny read! I started reading and was just sucked right in...a great mystery with twist and turns."
~ *Night Owl Reviews*

DANGER COVE BOOKS

Secret of the Painted Lady
Murder & Mai Tais
Death by Scones
Patchwork of Death
Deadly Dye & a Soy Chai
Killer Clue at the Ocean View
A Christmas Quilt to Die For
"A Killing in the Market"
(short story in the Killer Beach Reads collection)
Killer Colada
Passion, Poison, & Puppy Dogs
A Novel Death
Clues in Calico
Sinister Snickerdoodles
Heroes & Hurricanes
A Death in the Flower Garden
Divas, Diamonds & Death
A Slaying in the Orchard
A Secret in the Pumpkin Patch
Deadly Dirty Martinis
A Poison Manicure & Peach Liqueur
"Not-So-Bright Hopes"
(short story in the Pushing Up Daisies collection)
Tequila Trouble
Deadly Thanksgiving Sampler
Killer Eyeshadow & a Cold Espresso
Two Sleuths Are Better Than One
Dark Rum Revenge
Cozy Room With a Killer View

DEADLY DYE & A SOY CHAI

---

a Danger Cove mystery

Traci Andrighetti &
Elizabeth Ashby

DEADLY DYE AND A SOY CHAI

Published by Gemma Halliday Publishing

To my mom, Carolyn Andrighetti, for being my biggest fan, my fiercest critic, and a pretty darn good proofreader.

Acknowledgments

For as long as I'm writing books, I will begin every acknowledgements page by thanking Gemma Halliday. Not only did she hand me my career on a silver platter, so to speak, but she also asked me to write a series in the Danger Cove mysteries. To say that I am grateful to her is beyond inadequate.

When Gemma asked me to pick a type of business for my series, I immediately wanted to write about a hair salon. And I knew I could count on the best stylist and salon owner in Austin, Texas, to help me out—Debra Day at 4001 Duval Hair Salon. Thanks, Debra, for being my stylist, my friend, and now my consultant.

Two of my work buddies helped immensely with this book. When I was trying to come up with the plot, I wanted a unique murder weapon. So, *grazie*, Blaise Margherito for hissing the name of an awesome weapon at me—that one word inspired this entire novel. And *danke*, Andreas Hennen, for helping me with German language terms and food items for the character of Amy Spannagel.

As always, I need to thank Detective Ruben Vasquez from the Criminal Investigations Division of the Georgetown Police Department for suggesting and verifying proper police procedure. Although I have since had the good fortune to meet others in law enforcement at the Writers' Police Academy, Detective Vasquez is still my go-to source for all things police.

Of course, I would be remiss if I didn't thank my husband, Graham Kunze, for helping me to navigate the murky waters of the sailing world. I was practically drowning in a sea of bizarre and obscure sailing terminology until he rescued me. Speaking of family, I can't tell you how much I love and appreciate my super son, Dmitriy, for supporting me and for understanding why I have to go to bed so early every night.

CHAPTER ONE

"That statue's not wearing any panties!"

My body tensed at the outrage in Donna Bocca's voice. As the preeminent gossip of Danger Cove, not to mention a women's undergarment salesperson, she'd spread the news of this latest Conti family calamity all over town.

"And a child is watching," PTA member Mallory Winchester added through clenched teeth.

I stole a glance over my shoulder at the crowd gathering in the street. Besides Donna and Mallory, there was an elderly couple, an attractive thirty-something male with a camera, and Reverend Vickers's wife, Charlotte, with the members of her Bible study group. Even worse, a ten-year-old boy was speaking into a walkie-talkie with the intensity of a CIA agent on an intelligence-gathering mission.

I looked at my watch. It was a quarter after one on a Thursday in September. Why wasn't that kid in school?

I took a deep, calming breath of the crisp ocean air and then tried to convince myself that the situation wasn't really that bad. I mean, sure, there was a wooden statue of a gold rush era prostitute hovering, like a ghost of times past, from a rope in front of my home slash hair salon. And yes, she was skirtless and spread-eagle on a chair, displaying her intricately carved wares for all to see. But at least she had a shirt on.

"Beaver shot!" a young boy shouted.

I turned and saw packs of prepubescent males speeding up the sidewalk on bikes, alerted to the sex show, no doubt, by the CIA wannabe.

Okay, if little boys were ditching elementary school, then the situation *was* that bad.

I looked up on the roof. "Tucker," I began, trying to control the rising anxiety in my voice. "You need to get down and bring that statue with you. *Now*."

"Mellow out, Cassidi," he replied, giving me a half-lidded look. "I told you, the pulley's stuck."

Tucker Sloan was the owner of One Man's Trash, a junk shop on the outskirts of Danger Cove that dealt in antiques, used furniture, and eclectic decorative items, like my late Uncle Vincent Conti's—*ahem*—art collection. As Tucker's hippie-speak indicated, he was all about peace, love, and understanding. But right then, I wasn't about any of those things. When he'd bought the statue from me, he'd said that because of its "splayed style," it would be easier to move it out of a second-floor window than to try to take it down the spiral staircase. So much for that idea.

I cupped my hands around my mouth and whisper-shouted, "People are getting upset. Can't you unstick it?"

He shook his thick dreads. "Looks like old Sadie's not going to leave without a fight."

"Sadie?"

"Sexy Sadie's what your Uncle Vinnie used to call her. He nicknamed all of his women, real or otherwise." He grinned. "That cat was far out."

That was one way to describe him. "Could you please just try yanking the rope again?"

"Okay, but I don't think it'll do any good." Tucker braced himself with his legs and pulled until veins bulged in his neck and the fringe on his moccasins shook.

The pulley didn't budge, but Sadie did. She began to move back and forth like a swing. Each time she swung toward the street, the onlookers let out a collective gasp—and it wasn't because they were afraid that she was going to hit them.

"Seriously, Tucker?" I cried.

"I told you so, man," he replied.

I put my head in my hands—that is, until I heard one of the boys yell "Boobies!" followed by cheers from the rest of the under-twelve crowd.

I looked up and saw Tucker's temporary helper, Zac Taylor, pushing the ship's figurehead from my second-floor apartment out the double doors of the salon. It was also the likeness of a woman, but instead of baring her nether region, this one was baring her breasts. And Zac's face was buried right smack between them.

"That's a sight for sore eyes," a deep female voice said.

I turned and saw Amy Spannagel, the assistant librarian, dismounting her bike.

"You mean, an eyesore."

She pushed up her glasses. "I'm talking about Zac's ripped biceps. What are you talking about?"

I gave her a blank stare. For a PhD student, Amy could be kind of dense. But, as much as I hated to admit it, Zac's muscles were kind of distracting. Repairing boats at the Pirate's Hook Marine Services had done his body good. "I'm talking about my Uncle Vinnie's antique porn."

"It's not porn." She tucked a strand of mousy brown hair behind her ear. "It's art."

"Psh," I said with a flick of my hand. "You're from Seattle."

She arched her quasi unibrow. "So?"

"So, it's a lot more open minded than where I'm from. Trust me. In Fredericksburg, Texas, this stuff is straight-up smut. And apparently," I began, glancing back at the scowling faces in the crowd as Zac pulled the bare-breasted wench down the steps of the porch and into the yard, "it's smut in Danger Cove too."

Amy inclined her head to one side and nodded, conceding my porn point.

"Zac," Tucker shouted, "Sadie's putting up a fight. Come and give her a tug from below."

"Sure thing," he replied. "Just let me put Pearl on the truck."

"Who's Pearl?" Amy asked.

"That figurehead," Tucker replied. "She was the apple of Vinnie's eye."

I frowned at Pearl's cupless corset. "She's a real peach, all right."

Zac pushed Pearl up a ramp and into the bed of Tucker's old pickup. Then he walked between Sadie's legs, jumped up, and grabbed onto her thighs.

I was less than thrilled about the suggestive scene, but I was more than happy that he was blocking the va-jayjay view.

"Now that's what you call eye candy," Amy breathed, ogling the backside of Zac's tight jeans.

"Hello!" I gave her a shove.

"What?" She lurched to the side and stumbled out of a penny loafer.

"I'm trying to clean up the image of The Clip and Sip and the Conti family name, and your gawking isn't helping."

Avoiding my gaze, Amy put her shoe on and pulled her socks high, as though suddenly ashamed of her naked knees.

"She's starting to drop," Zac announced as he let go of Sadie's massive thighs. But instead of lowering to the ground, she began to rock left and right.

The little boys began whistling and fist pumping like budding wannabe strip-club patrons.

"Sadie sure is kicking up a fuss," Tucker commented.

"She's kicking, all right," I yelled. "A burlesque version of the cancan."

No sooner had I spoken than a woman in the crowd let out a muffled cry.

Amy turned toward the street. "Looks like Charlotte Vickers just went down."

I threw my hands in the air. "That's it," I shouted. "Cut the rope."

"But Sadie's over a hundred and fifty years old," Tucker protested. "She might not survive the fall."

"Then you can take comfort in the fact that she's had a good, long life." I pointed at the offending item. "Now, you promised me that this would be a quick job, so you've got ten more minutes to get this junk off my property."

Tucker pulled a pocketknife from the front pouch of his Mexican Baja jacket and began cutting. "This is a real drag, man."

After a few seconds, the rope snapped, and Sadie hit the ground. But she didn't have the decency to fall on her face. She landed upright, lascivious grin and all.

Tucker hurried down the ladder and ran to Sadie's side. After he was sure that her parts were intact, he breathed a sigh of relief. "Groovy."

"Yeah, outtasight." I put my hands on my hips. "You dig?"

His face was expressionless. Then a light went on in his burned-out brain. "Grab a leg, Zac. Let's get Sadie on the truck."

Zac ran a hand through his thick, brown hair and flashed me a mischievous smile. "Did you want us to take Hope, Faith, and Charity too?"

My face turned as pink as my Blushing Berry lip gloss. He was referring to a painting-sized photograph from the late 1800s of three prostitutes on their backs with legs splayed, clothed only in socks and shoes.

"We'd be happy to take them off your hands," he added, winking a sexy, steel-blue eye.

"I'm sure you would," I intoned as he turned to help Tucker with Sadie.

"Hey," Amy said, punching my arm.

"Ow." I glared at her as I rubbed my bicep. "What did you do that for?"

"Because you promised me that picture."

"You can have it. But why would you want that hideous thing?"

"It's vintage erotica." She adjusted her beige cardigan. "And not everyone can have blonde hair and a petite figure like you. Some of us girls need a little help with the opposite sex."

I pretended to be absorbed in the loading of Sadie onto the truck. Amy and I had become friends a couple of months ago when I started studying for my online accounting class at the library. And if there was one thing I'd learned (it wasn't accounting), it was that she liked to talk about her nonexistent love life. As much as I wanted to be there for her, now wasn't the time. I had a staff meeting to plan and a quiz to study for. Besides, truth be told, talking about Amy's man troubles reminded me of mine, and that was something I'd rather forget.

"The girls are ready to go," Tucker said as Zac slammed the door of the truck bed shut. "Later, Cassidi."

Now that Sadie and Pearl were covered by a tarp, I turned to the sizable crowd. "Peep show's over, folks."

The townspeople began to disperse, and Tucker climbed into the driver's seat and started the engine. Zac saluted and got into the truck.

"Wait," I said, approaching the passenger door. "How much do I owe you for helping Tucker move the, uh, things?"

He leaned out the window. "Nothing. I used to work for Tucker in high school, so I was happy to help." He paused. "Especially since it meant coming to your place."

Flustered by his comment, I pulled some cash from the pocket of my jeans. "I insist."

"Okay." He gave an opportunist smile. "Then how about dinner?"

I felt my face flush. "I…I'd rather pay you for your time." I shoved three twenties into his hand. "That should cover it."

He looked from the money to me. "For now."

I nodded and then did a double take when I processed what he'd said. But before I could respond, Tucker flashed the peace sign out the driver's window and sped away.

"Can you believe that Zac guy?" I asked as I stared after the truck.

Amy punched me in the arm—again. "He was hitting on you."

"*You're* hitting on me," I corrected. "What's up with you today?"

"Someone has to knock some sense into you." She put her hand on her hip. "Zac Taylor is one of the most sought-after guys in town. You owe it to those of us who'll never get a date with him to go for it."

I crossed my arms. "I told you. I'm not interested in dating right now."

She looked me straight in the eyes. "It's because of whatever happened between you and that guy back in Fredericksburg, isn't it?"

"That has nothing to do with it," I fibbed, wishing I'd never alluded to the unfortunate incident. "You know that between the hair salon and my class, I've got more on my plate than I can handle."

"That reminds me," Amy said as she reached into her messenger bag. "Here's that textbook you wanted."

"Thanks." I took the accounting tome, and the sheer weight of it served as a reminder of the burden of school. "If I don't make a C or better on that quiz in the morning, I'll have to drop the course."

"You can do it." Amy straddled her bike in her blue pencil skirt. "Are we still on for girls' night tomorrow?"

"Absolutely." I frowned at the textbook. "Pass or fail, I'm going to need to get my drink on. This has been a hard week, and the statue striptease just now didn't help."

She wrinkled her forehead. "Is everything okay?"

I shrugged. "Business has been especially bad. I can count the number of clients that Lucy, Gia, and I've had on two hands."

"Well, you've only been in town for a few months. The customers will come."

"Yeah." I stared at the pink-and-orange plaid pattern on my shirt. "I'm sure they will."

Amy looked at her watch. "My lunch hour's almost up. I'd better get back to the library."

"'K. See you tomorrow night." I watched Amy ride away and wondered whether the customers really would come. In the four months that I'd been in Danger Cove, I'd gotten a real education, and it had nothing to do with my degree. The people of the town were nice but wary of me and my salon. And now that I knew why, I couldn't say that I blamed them. As much as I'd wanted to escape small-town Texas, I might have stayed put if I'd known the truth about Uncle Vinnie and this building.

* * *

I stared at the bank balance on my laptop screen. That couldn't be right, could it? The clock was showing the correct time, 2:30 p.m., so my computer was working properly. I blinked in case something was clouding my vision. Nope, still the same number. I tried closing my weak eye, but it was no use. Any way

I looked at it, I had three months of money before my inheritance from Uncle Vinnie ran out. I sighed and rested my head on the back of the wooden chair.

"I hear I missed quite a show today," my step-cousin, Gia Di Mitri, said from the doorway of the salon break room.

I turned my head to glare at her but winced instead. I didn't know which was more blinding—the afternoon sun shining through the bay window or Gia's bright-blue stretch top, pink cheetah-print tights, and neon-yellow stilettos. "Who told you that?"

"Woman Mouth," she replied, translating Donna Bocca's name from Italian. "I was shopping at Lily's Lingerie when she came in for her shift. She told everyone in the store that the statue gave Zac Taylor a lap dance." She opened the refrigerator and pulled out a can of lemon soda. "Which is pretty funny if you think about it."

"Yeah. Hilarious." Despite my sarcasm, I *could* see the humor. It was a tragic comedy.

Gia popped the tab on the can and flopped into a chair. "Just remember, Cass, there's no such thing as bad publicity."

"No?" I spread my arms to emphasize the emptiness of the salon.

Lucy O'Connell rushed into the room, her curly red tendrils flying. "Sorry I'm late," she said as she took a seat at the table. "Since we didn't have any clients, I babysat for Mallory Winchester while she ran an errand, but it took longer than she expected." She bit her lip. "She said it was because she had to stop by here to see your porno yard sale with her own two eyes."

"Yard sale?" Now I took offense to that but not to the "porno" part. I was hardly the type to sell the girls—and by that I mean "the merchandise"—on the front lawn.

Gia's shiny lips straightened into a flat line. "Yeah, I'll bet she wanted to see it—every square inch."

"Oh, Mallory wouldn't have any interest in those statues," Lucy said. "She's into Pennsylvania Dutch art."

Gia rolled her eyes.

"Let's just start the meeting," I interjected. As upset as I was about Mallory's take on the event, I had to brush it off—just like I'd brushed off the news that the Victorian home I lived and worked in had a hundred-year history as a brothel for local lumberjacks. "Now," I began, glancing at my notes, "the plan is still to grow The Clip and Sip to fill the three empty salon chairs and hire a receptionist, despite the lack of customers."

Lucy cleared her throat. "Yeah, about that…"

I looked up.

"Um, if business doesn't pick up soon…"

"Yeah?" Gia prodded, tapping the silver-glittered tips of her French-manicured nails on the table.

Lucy looked like a deer caught in the headlights. "Well, I'll have to find another job."

My heart sank. I couldn't lose Lucy. I'd had to lure Gia from New Jersey with the promise of free room and board after Lucy was the only hairstylist in Danger Cove who'd answered my ad. "I understand."

"I'm sorry," Lucy said, big blue eyes welling with tears. "It's just that I won't ever be able to save enough money to marry Sven."

Sven Mattsun was a Swedish exchange student from Stockholm whom Lucy had fallen head over heels for two years ago during their senior year at Danger Cove High School. Ever since he'd returned home last year, Lucy had been scrimping and saving to pay for her to move to Sweden and their wedding.

Gia snorted. "What do you really know about the Swedish Fish, anyway?"

"Gia!" I scolded. "Sven's not a piece of candy."

"Too bad for Lucy," she said, examining a lock of her hair for split ends.

Lucy's chin trembled. "I know that I love him, no matter what you think."

Gia tossed the lock of hair to the side and shook her head.

"I met Sven when he came for a visit, and he's very nice," I said in a soothing tone for Lucy's benefit. Then I turned to Gia. "He's way better than those brainless bodybuilder types you go for. They can barely carry on a conversation."

She flipped her silky black hair over her shoulder. "Who needs to talk?"

I smirked. "Men aren't just for sex, you know."

"Who said anything about sex? I just meant that men aren't exactly known for their conversational skills."

She had me there. "Give it a little more time, Lucy. I have some ideas to bring in more business."

"Really?" Her eyes widened. "Like what?"

"For starters, The Clip and Sip now serves alcohol." I handed each of them a copy of the new drink menu. "Every customer gets either a free glass of wine or one of my homemade liqueurs."

Lucy's face brightened. "This is awesome. It'll feel more like a spa experience."

Gia took a sip of soda as she perused the drink list. "And a little Texas moonshine might help to alleviate the bitter taste in people's mouths about the building's past."

I shot her a look. "Peach liqueur hardly qualifies as moonshine. Anyway, Gia, you'll also offer a complimentary manicure to our customers."

She dropped the menu. "How will I get paid?"

"I'll have to cover your commission during the promotion." I couldn't afford it, but it was the least I could do. Even though my aunt Carla had married Gia's father, Frank, ten years before when we were both sixteen, my Uncle Vinnie hadn't left Gia so much as a mention in his will. Apparently, he hadn't been as into family as my dad, Domenic. But now that I thought about it, ever since my dad had divorced my mom last year and moved back to his native New Jersey, he didn't seem too interested in family, either, because I'd hardly heard from him since.

Gia patted me on the back. "Thanks, Cass."

"Also," I began, "since we're so close to Seattle, we're going to offer coffee drinks. I bought a professional-grade espresso machine by Nuova Simonelli."

"Those are like twelve grand!" Gia exclaimed. "I knew your Uncle Vinnie was loaded."

"He wasn't. I bought the machine on credit." My stomach turned as I admitted that last part. "Anyway, I'm glad you're excited about the machine, because you're going to make the drinks."

"I'm going to make cawffee too?" she squawked, her New Jersey accent rearing its colorful head. "Why do all of your new promotions involve me?"

"Because you have skills that Lucy and I don't," I replied. "Plus, your makeup services haven't exactly taken off."

Her eyes narrowed. "It's not my fault that the nature-loving ladies of Danger Cove don't appreciate the smoky eye."

The smoky eye was the unofficial state look of New Jersey. But the combination of purple, blue, and even green eye shadow with smudged eyeliner would be more appropriately named "the sickly eye." "No, but it is your fault that you don't apply makeup that's suited to the client."

"But the whole point of makeup is to look made up, not"—she wrinkled her mouth—"*natural.*"

"The *whole point* is to make the client happy," I snapped. "Now, starting today, we're running an ad about our new services in the *Cove Chronicles*. In the meantime, I need the two of you to spread the word, especially you, Lucy. Tell all of your girlfriends and their moms."

She nodded. "I'm sorry to bring this up, but…"

Gia exhaled loudly. "For crying out loud—just spit it out."

"Is there any update on getting the ceiling fixed?"

Gia and I exchanged a look.

"I know it's a sensitive subject," Lucy continued, "and I wouldn't normally bring it up, but it's starting to sag. And since it's right above my chair…"

I shifted in my seat. "Well, I'll have to get police permission for a plumber to go into Uncle Vinnie's room. I can stop by the station today."

"Thanks, Cassidi."

An uncomfortable silence fell over the room.

Gia turned to me and cocked a well-plucked brow. "Is that it?"

I looked at my meeting agenda. "That's all I have."

"No, I mean, is that all you have planned to bring in new clients? Because, if you ask me, we need something bigger."

Of course, I hadn't asked Gia, but I knew from experience that she was going to tell me exactly what she thought. "What do you have in mind?"

"Egypt." Her face beamed brighter than her outfit.

I blinked. "I'm not following you."

Gia stood up and started to pace. "Think Cleopatra, the most regal and seductive queen of all time."

"O-kay," I said.

"We want to make women feel like her. You know, spread out all sexy on a gold chaise lounge."

I was pretty sure that the chaise lounge was a modern French invention, but whatever.

"So, picture this," Gia continued, motioning like a movie director. "We give the clients blowouts. But instead of the smoky eye, we do the Cleopatra eye. And the whole time they're in the chair, tanned bodybuilders are fanning them with those big feather-duster things and feeding them with their hands."

I stared at Gia openmouthed, and Lucy went pale.

"You do realize, don't you, that using sex to sell the salon is exactly what I *don't* want to do?" I paused for effect. "For obvious reasons."

"Gawd!" Gia threw her head back in frustration. "Sex sells, Cassidi. It sold when this place was a brothel, and it sold when your Uncle Vinnie ran his hair salon here. That's why his business was so successful."

"Yes." I met her gaze straight on. "But that's also what got him murdered."

CHAPTER TWO

Gia was the first to speak. "You don't know that Vinnie's death had anything to do with sex."

"Oh, no?" I arched a brow. "Then how do you explain the black fishnet stocking around his neck? The one with the red sequin heart appliqué?"

"Don't forget the black silk ribbon," Lucy added with a nod.

"That doesn't prove he was with a woman," Gia said with a shooing motion. "Maybe a jealous husband strangled him."

I crossed my arms. "Still sex related."

Gia flipped her hair. "Well, even if it was, he was living the life. You know, that whole 'wine, women, and song' thing that old people always talk about. And he told my stepmom that business was so good, he already had enough money to retire."

"Maybe he was trying to impress Aunt Carla," I said. Because the amount he'd left me was only enough to keep afloat for about six months.

The salon bell sounded.

"That must be Margaret Appleby," Lucy said, rising to her feet.

Gia grimaced. "You mean, Miss Marple."

"Lower your voice," I whispered.

Lucy grabbed the new drink menu. "I'll take this out to her."

I turned to Gia. "Margaret has been coming here since Uncle Vinnie owned the salon. Please be polite to her."

"Fine," she huffed. "But, blue hair aside, that woman is straight out of an Agatha Christie movie."

"Novel," I corrected. "And she's one of the sweetest ladies I've ever met."

"I agree, but it totally creeps me out when she takes a nap under the hair dryer. She looks like she's dead."

"Give her a break, will you? She's eighty years old."

"I know." Gia gave me a pointed look. "But I get that bad feeling every time she comes in."

I sighed. Ever since Gia had predicted that my relationship with my ex, Shane Austin, would end badly—a fact that the entire town of Fredericksburg had also foreseen—she thought that she had psychic powers. "I don't care if you get a stabbing feeling—you're going to greet her with a smile. Because if I go under, you go under. *Capish*?"

Gia's mouth opened in outrage as she shot to her feet. "Sometimes you're *such* a prima donna."

Oh, the irony.

As I entered the salon, I smiled at the stooped woman sitting in Lucy's chair. "Hi, Ms. Appleby. Have you had time to look over our new drink menu?"

"Why, yes." Her blue eyes twinkled. "I'll have a chai latte, dear. But with soy. I can't tolerate milk, you know." She squeezed my forearm with knobby, arthritic fingers. "Gives me gas."

Gia wrinkled her nose as if she smelled said gas. "I'll get right on it."

The door opened, and a cute, athletic-looking brunette entered. "Do you take walk-ins?" She smiled and raised a hand to her bob. "My bangs could use a trim."

"Absolutely." I tried to hide my excitement as I ushered her to the station beside Lucy's. "Welcome to The Clip and Sip. I'm Cassidi."

She slipped out of her sailing jacket and sat in the chair. "Prudence Miller."

"Can I get you something to drink?" I asked, putting the cape around her. "We have tea, coffee, wine, and homemade liqueurs."

"I'd love a glass of Pinot Grigio, if you've got it."

"Coming right up." I looked at Gia, who had just handed Margaret her soy chai. She glowered and headed back to the break room.

"I haven't seen you around town," I said as I turned on the water and waited for it to warm up. "Are you new to Danger Cove?"

"Just passing through. I took a leave of absence from my job in LA to sail my boat to Alaska."

"Wow, that's quite an adventure," I said in awe of her bravery. It had taken all the courage I could muster—and a couple of Xanax—to move to a ready-made house and business in Danger Cove. I wouldn't dream of sailing a boat that far on my own—not for all the oil money in Texas.

I lowered the chair backward and began to wet her hair, and she closed her eyes as the warm water ran over her head.

I studied her face for a moment. She was a dead ringer for Kate Jackson back in the 1980s. "What type of work do you do?"

"Hospital administration."

"Well, I'm jealous." I shut off the water and applied shampoo. "The beaches here in Washington are nowhere near as warm and sunny as the ones in California."

She laughed. "Actually, I'm not much of a beach bum. I'm always too busy sailing."

"Believe it or not, I learned how to sail in Texas," I said as I worked the shampoo into a lather. My mind drifted to the lazy summers I'd spent with Shane on Lake Travis, and then I promptly squashed those memories. "I did it for a guy, of course."

The corners of her mouth turned up. "I think that's how a lot of women get into sailing."

I turned on the faucet and began rinsing her hair. "What about you?" I asked, trying to keep the conversation going. "Did you learn to sail in LA?"

"No, on Cape Cod where I grew up," she said quietly. "There, learning to sail is almost as common as learning to drive."

Sensing that Prudence was tiring of the polite chatter, I let her relax in peace while I continued to rinse. Then I wrapped a towel around her head and raised the chair to an upright position just as Gia returned with the wine.

"I really need this," Prudence said as she took the glass.

Gia put on her poker face. "Don't we all."

As I removed a sanitized comb from the canister, the bell on the salon door sounded.

I glanced at the door and recognized Bertha Braun, a retired nurse and lifelong bachelorette in her late seventies whom I'd met during a marketing call at the Senior Citizen Center.

"I'm here to see your makeup artist," Bertha announced, striking a pose in the lobby. "And I'm going to need some of that scrumptious Italian strawberry liqueur you make, Cassidi. What's it called? Frog-something?"

"*Fragolino*," I replied, suppressing a smile.

"You got it," Gia exclaimed as she practically ran to the break room—clearly thrilled to have her own client.

Bertha's eyes zeroed in on Margaret. "I have a date tonight," she said at the top of her lungs as she sashayed to the chair behind Lucy's. "We're going to the Lobster Pot, so I want to look extra special."

"Better get out the war paint," Margaret suggested sweetly before taking a sip from her teacup.

Lucy, who'd been stirring the blue rinse for Margaret's hair, stopped in midmix and shot me a look of surprise, while Prudence sipped her wine and looked on amused.

Bertha showed no sign of having heard the comment, and I was grateful. Her nickname around town was Bulldog, both because of her dogged personality and her barrel-chested body type. And the last thing I needed at the salon was an elderly throwdown.

"In that case, Bertha," Gia began, returning in record time with a cordial glass full of the red liqueur, "you'll want Mad Makeup. It's my personal line that I designed to celebrate the glamour of New Jersey."

Yeah, because the Garden State has long been known as the center of haute couture, I thought as I clipped Prudence's bangs.

"Oh, that sounds exotic," Bertha cooed. "Just like my date. Maybe you know him?" She looked behind her to see whether Margaret was paying attention. "Santiago Beltrán?"

At the mention of his name, Margaret straightened in her chair.

"Never heard of him," Gia said as she opened her eye shadow case. "But he sounds like a real Latin Lover."

Bertha's thin, wrinkled lips spread into a lizard-like smile. "That's because he's Cuban."

"Well in that case, I think we should go with a strong look." Gia tapped her index finger on her cheek. "Something militaristic."

While Gia elaborated on her plans for Bertha, I had to bite my lip to focus on Prudence's hair. If you asked me, Mad Makeup should have been named Commando Cosmetics. The colors included raging reds, bellicose blues, and glaring greens—there wasn't a pastel in the palette. The line also had alarming accessories, like camouflage eye makeup stickers and temporary lip tattoos. It was hardly a style appropriate for a quaint cove town.

Bertha took a gulp of her *fragolino*. "That sounds perfect. Santiago's very macho, just like his famous countryman, Ricardo Montalbán."

Margaret snorted, causing her turkey neck to wobble. "Ricardo Montalbán is Mexican. If anyone, Santiago is like Ricky Ricardo."

"You mean, Desi Arnaz," Bertha corrected.

"No, I mean Ricky Ricardo, because you're going to drive poor Santiago crazy, just like Lucy did Ricky." Margaret smirked. "After one date with you, he'll run screaming 'Babalú.'"

Bertha's face grew dark, thanks only in part to Gia's handiwork. "You're just jealous. Tell us, Margaret. Exactly how many dates have you had in the thirty-odd years you've lived in Danger Cove?"

"Just one," she replied, grinning like a Cheshire cat. "But it was enough to last me a lifetime."

"Hogwash," Bertha spat. "Who was it with?"

Margaret met Bertha's eyes in the mirror. "Vincent Conti."

I gasped and narrowly missed lopping off one side of Prudence's bangs. My Uncle Vinnie was fifty-five when he died, which made him almost thirty years younger than Margaret Appleby. Surely what they'd shared had just been a…a friendly lunch?

"I don't believe that for a minute," Bertha scoffed. "What would a handsome stud like that want with an old crone like you?"

"To have his way with me, apparently." Margaret drained the last of her soy chai, as though the steamy memory left her parched. "Talk about a Latin Lover. Vincent was my Marcello Mastroianni. He even had a tattoo on that tight little tush of his that said 'La Dolce Vita.'"

Everyone in the room was struck speechless, and I had to lean on my station to steady myself. *Looks like they'd shared a lot more than lunch.*

"It's a shame he's gone," Margaret continued in the stunned silence. "I don't suppose you have any more uncles, dear?"

I stared at her open-mouthed. Was Margaret some kind of man-eater?

"No, just her aunt Carla, my stepmom," Gia intervened. "Unless you count her dad, Domenic."

"W-we're p-pretty small by Italian family standards," I stammered as I searched for some way to bring the sexual conversation away from my father. "Um, what about you, Prudence? Are you from a big family?"

"I'm the only child of two only children," she replied. "So, it was pretty lonely growing up."

Margaret frowned. "The important thing is that you had two parents who loved you, dear."

Prudence nodded. "So true."

Relieved that the conversation was on safer ground, I took one last snip from Prudence's bangs and picked up my hair dryer.

"Oh, I always let my hair dry naturally," she said as she pulled cash from her front pocket. "How much do I owe you?"

"Forty bucks," I replied.

Prudence took one last sip of her Pinot Grigio and then handed me fifty dollars. "Thanks, Cassidi."

"Thank *you*," I replied as I escorted her to the door. "Enjoy your stay in Danger Cove."

"Definitely." She grinned. "This place is an answer to my prayers."

Let's hope it's an answer to mine, I thought as I closed the door. I turned and saw Bertha climb from Gia's chair with two green, black, and brown eyes and a nonexistent mouth. She looked like she was ready to embark on the Bay of Pigs Invasion.

"Always remember the Jersey rule," Gia advised. "Go with a nude lip—at the most, pale pink. The only thing you want to accentuate is the eyes, especially for a romantic dinner."

"Oh, I agree," Bertha said. "Now I need to be on my way, or I won't have enough time to get ready."

"Then your date had better be next year," Margaret said as Lucy helped her take a seat beneath a dryer, "because it's going to take at least that long to make a battle-ax like you look presentable."

Bertha balled her fists at her sides, and her face turned so red that it was visible through her pancake makeup. "Lucky for you I'm in a good mood today," she said in a dangerously low voice. "Otherwise, I would shut that miserable trap of yours once and for all."

Margaret's mouth formed an *O* shape in mock alarm, but Lucy's fear was real. She turned white and stepped out of Bertha's way.

"Ladies, please," I said with my arms outstretched. "Let's keep it civil."

"I should go," Bertha said with jagged breath. She tossed back the rest of her liqueur, handed several bills to Gia, and stormed to the door. Before leaving, she spun around and glared at Margaret. "For your sake, Cassidi, I hope the quality of your clientele improves."

I watched Bertha stomp from the salon and wondered whether she would ever come back. I sighed and followed Gia into the break room.

"You think Miss Appleby's telling the truth about Vinnie?" she asked as she threw her fuchsia bag over her shoulder.

"I'd rather not think about it," I said as I washed my hands in the sink. I heard a jangling sound and turned to see Gia holding the keys to the sleek, black Ferrari California that I'd inherited along with the property. "Are you taking the car?"

"Why, do you need it?" she asked as though it had come as a complete surprise to her that I might want to use our only means of transportation.

"The unpleasant exchange between Margaret and Bertha reminded me that I have an unpleasant errand to run," I replied in a bitter tone. "Could you drop me off at the police station?"

"Of course." Gia slipped on oversized white sunglasses. "But don't let the biddy brawl get you down. Remember what I said about publicity."

I rolled my eyes.

Lucy entered with Margaret's cup and saucer. "You're leaving?"

"I'll be back in an hour," I said as I grabbed my jean jacket from the back of the chair. "Hold down the fort."

"And if Bertha comes back for the blue-haired broad," Gia added, "man the artillery."

Lucy's eyes grew wide, and I pushed Gia from the break room.

As we made our way to the door, I glanced at Margaret. She was resting under the warmth of the dryer with her eyes closed and her hands folded in her lap. The corners of her mouth formed a small smile. I wondered whether she was reminiscing about her altercation with Bertha or her rendezvous with my uncle. I wanted to believe that it was the former. I'd never really known my Uncle Vinnie, but I'd been told that he was "the black sheep of our family." I was finally starting to understand why.

* * *

I turned my accounting textbook sideways, hoping that a new perspective would help me to make sense of the information. As I scrutinized the numbers, a shadow fell over the page. I looked up and saw the hulking figure of Detective Bud Ohlsen.

"Were you waiting to see me, Miss Conti?"

"Yessir, Detective, sir," I said, using my Texas police manners. Not that I'd had a lot of experience with the law—just a speeding ticket or two. Okay, and an underage drinking charge. "I'd like to talk to you about my uncle, Vincent Conti's, case."

He ran a hand through his salt-and-pepper hair. "I've got to run down to the pier. Can you come back in a couple of hours?"

"I'm not sure. I share a car with my cousin, and she dropped me off—"

"I'd be happy to drive you home," he interrupted. "We could talk on the way?"

"Thank you. This won't take long." I closed my book and followed him outside to the parking lot behind the station.

To my relief, he led me to an unmarked car. I wasn't relishing the thought of being spotted by the likes of Donna Bocca or Mallory Winchester in the company of the Danger Cove police so soon after the statue screw up. "I can sit in the front, right?"

He pursed his lips. "Unless you've done something I don't know about."

"Nossir, Detective." I hopped into the passenger seat and tried to wipe the guilt from my face. I hadn't done anything wrong, but dealing with the police always made me feel like I had.

Detective Ohlsen lowered himself into the car and pulled the seat belt over his wide midsection before starting the ignition. "Now, what was it you wanted to talk to me about?"

"There's a water leak coming from my uncle's old bathroom, and it's damaging the ceiling above one of the salon chairs. If we don't get the pipe fixed soon, I'm afraid the sheetrock will collapse on a client."

"What makes you think the leak is coming from his bathroom?" he asked as he pulled onto the street. "If I remember correctly, there are sinks in all the upstairs bedrooms."

I shifted uncomfortably. The sinks were a not-so-charming feature from the building's brothel days, since they served as a one-stop freshen-up spot between clients, if you know what I mean. Fortunately, the LaSalle House, as the brothel was known, finally went out of business in 1955 when a group of God-fearing women (i.e., prostitute-loathing wives) set fire to the place. What remained of the building had been abandoned for forty years, until my uncle had turned the bottom floor into a hair salon and restored the top floor to its former, uh, glory. "Yeah, but the damage is right below the sink in his bathroom."

"I see." Detective Ohlsen chewed his cheek as he slowed to a stop at a red light.

I waited for him to say something. When he didn't, I cleared my throat. "Would it be all right to have a plumber come out and fix the leak?"

He exhaled. "Your uncle's room is no longer an active crime scene, but since the investigation is still ongoing, we'd like to keep it as intact as possible." He glanced at me. "You're not using the room, are you?"

"Me?" I shuddered. "Oh, no way, sir. I mean, Detective. I keep it locked at all times."

"Good." He hit the gas. "Because there's certainly no shortage of bedrooms in the place."

"So," I began, eager to shift the conversation away from all those sinks and bedrooms, "does that mean I can't call a plumber?"

He hooked a left onto Fletcher Way. "Make an appointment, and let me know the date and time. I'll send an officer out to keep contamination to a minimum."

I stiffened. The last thing The Clip and Sip needed right now was a cop car out front. "I don't suppose that there's anyway you could send someone in an unmarked car?"

"I'll see what I can do."

"Thanks." At least there was some good news where the salon was concerned, but I was starting to wonder whether there was ever going to be any good news for my family and me about my Uncle Vinnie's homicide investigation. "I don't suppose there've been any developments in the case?"

"Something has come to our attention, yes." He fell silent.

I'd heard that Detective Ohlsen was a man of few words, so I pressed on, desperate for some information about my uncle's murder. "Can you tell me about it?"

"Vinnie's former receptionist said they often got strange calls from clients."

"Strange how?"

"That part's privileged." He slowed the car to a stop in front of the salon.

"I understand." I opened the car door. "You know, I really appreciate your work on the case. I didn't really know my Uncle Vinnie, but his death has really taken a toll on me and my whole family. And honestly, if it's not solved soon, I'm not sure what will become of the salon. Or of me, for that matter."

He turned to face me. "If you don't mind my asking, Miss Conti, why *would* you want to live and operate a business on the site where your uncle was murdered?"

Detective Ohlsen wasn't the first person to ask me that question. I took a deep breath and decided to tell him the truth. After all, he was a cop. "I kind of made a mess of my life back home. And just when I was thinking that I needed a do-over, I inherited a home and a business in another state. All things considered, I figured it was a pretty sweet deal for a twenty-six-year-old."

"I imagine so." He nodded. "Good day, Miss Conti."

"Bye, Detective. And thanks for the ride." I stepped out of the car and walked up the sidewalk to the old Victorian building, wondering for around the hundredth time whether it really was such a sweet deal.

There was no direct entrance to my house upstairs, so I decided to enter through the front door of the salon and see whether Lucy needed help closing up shop. As I pulled open the door, I glanced at the time on my phone. It was almost five o'clock, which meant that I had the evening to study for my quiz. And I was going to need every minute of it.

I shoved my phone back into my bag and looked around the salon. There was no sign of Lucy, but Margaret was still dozing beneath the dryer. Apparently, the caffeine in the soy chai latte hadn't been enough to keep her from that date with her afternoon nap.

"Date" turned out to be a poor choice of words because I got an instant visual of Margaret and Uncle Vinnie locked in a passionate embrace. I shook my head to dispel the icky image and grabbed the mail from the reception desk as a distraction. But the stack of bills was an equally sickening sight.

I tossed the mail back onto the desk and headed to the break room. Like it or not, it was time to hit the books. But before I could do that, I had to find Lucy. She needed to wake up Margaret before the dye dried out her hair.

"Lucy?" I peered into the room.

But she wasn't there. Nor was she on the back porch or in the bathroom adjoining the break room.

I was starting to get concerned. Lucy wouldn't leave during the middle of an appointment, especially not when she was the only stylist in the salon.

"First things first," I muttered as I walked out to the dryers. "Time to rinse your hair, Ms. Appleby."

As usual, she didn't budge.

I bent over and reached out to shake her, but then my hand recoiled. And I blinked—hard.

Because either my eyes were playing tricks on me, or Margaret Appleby had turned the exact same shade of blue as her hair.

CHAPTER THREE

I let out a scream that would wake the dead. But it didn't wake Margaret Appleby.

Lucy ran from the break room, holding her cell phone. "What is it? Are the statues back?"

I gaped at her, astonished. How could she think that the statues would cause my bloodcurdling scream? But the truth was that if Tucker were to return Sadie and Pearl, I would scream blue murder—I mean, *bloody* murder. "Call 9-1-1! Margaret's unconscious."

Lucy's finger trembled as she tapped the numbers on her phone.

"Where were you? I looked everywhere."

She put the phone to her ear, and her teeth began to chatter. "I-in the p-pine trees out back. Sven called, and we got into a fight. I-I didn't want Margaret to hear."

I looked at Margaret's lifeless body and doubled over. The nausea was starting, and so was the dizziness. I was about to have a panic attack. But I couldn't let that happen, not now. I had to try to resuscitate Margaret. The problem was that I didn't have the faintest idea how. "Do you know CPR?"

Lucy shook her head and held up her hand to silence me. "W-we need a-an ambulance at 627 Fletcher Way," she stammered into the receiver. "Th-there's been a-an accident with an elderly client."

By now the room was beginning to tilt, so I did the 5-2-5 breathing exercise I'd been taught to ease my anxiety. I inhaled for five counts, held my breath for two, exhaled for five.

"Hang on." Lucy pulled the phone from her face. "What are Margaret's symptoms?"

"Can't you see that she's blue?" I yelled at the top of my air-filled lungs. "People who turn blue aren't breathing, right?"

So much for that calming technique.

Lucy listened to the 9-1-1 operator, and then her mouth contracted in horror. "Oh, no," she wailed. "I-I can't touch her. She looks…d-d-dead."

Okay, so Lucy wasn't good in a crisis either. It was time to pull myself together. After all, I was the owner of the salon, and a client's life depended on me. "What are they telling you to do?"

"Lay her flat and do mouth-to-mouth."

I slipped off my jean jacket. "Grab Margaret's feet and help me lower her to the floor."

Lucy laid her phone on the floor. Beads of sweat formed on her upper lip as we struggled to lift Margaret from the chair and place her on the floor.

"Talk about dead weight," I muttered. I realized the magnitude of what I'd said only after I saw Lucy's stricken face. "I didn't mean it that way," I soothed as I put my jacket beneath Margaret's head. "She's going to be fine."

Lucy swallowed. "What do we do now?"

"Whatever the 9-1-1 operator tells us," I replied with a calmness I didn't feel. "You listen to the instructions and repeat them to me. Understand?"

She nodded and put the phone to her ear. "She's on the floor. We're ready for the next step."

The salon bell buzzed as the door burst open.

"What?" Gia spread her arms wide. "So now we're making Sleeping Beauty a pallet on the floor?"

"Shh!" I hissed. "Lucy's talking to 9-1-1. Something's wrong with Margaret."

Since silence wasn't a skill Gia practiced, she scurried over in her stilettos, removed her supersized sunglasses, and squinted at Margaret. "Holy freakin' cannoli. If she were a guy, she could join the Blue Man Group."

I shot her a look of death. "Can you please cut the jokes and help us? This is serious."

"Who's joking?" Gia exclaimed. "The woman looks like Nanny Smurf. What'd she do? Drink her hair dye?"

"Of course not!" I snapped, although I had my doubts, given Margaret's blue hue. "She stopped breathing."

"Then why are yous just sittin' there?" she exclaimed in New Jerseyese. "Start chest compressions!"

I gasped. "*You* know CPR?"

Gia fell to her knees and ripped the cape from Margaret. "I worked as a barista in Atlantic City, remember?"

"So?"

"Do you know how many hipsters OD on artisanal coffee?" she asked as she began pumping Margaret's chest.

I made a mental note to monitor the coffee intake of my customers, especially those wearing hats, scarves, and skinny jeans. Then I remembered that soy chai latte. Was it possible that the small amount of caffeine in the tea had stopped Margaret's heart?

"CPR is underway," Lucy said into the receiver. Then, seemingly without thinking, she ended the call and clutched the phone to her chest.

As Gia alternated between pumps and breaths, I examined Margaret. She had a bluish tint to her lips and skin, like she'd been stained by blue ink—or blue dye. Even her yellowed fingernails had turned a pale shade of blue, which made my stomach lurch. The rinse Lucy had used was designed to take the yellow out of gray hair. So, was Gia right? Had Margaret somehow ingested the dye?

The sound of sirens and the ringing phone shook me from my thoughts. "Lucy, that's probably 9-1-1 calling you back."

She jumped and pressed Answer. "Hello?"

I watched her carefully. She was kind of fragile, and I was worried that this situation would be too much for her to handle.

"Yes, they've arrived," Lucy said, and then she hung up again.

"Lucy, what happened after Gia and I left?"

Her eyes grew to the size of saucers. "You don't think I—"

"I don't know what to think," I interrupted. "That's why I'm asking you for answers."

"But you were here when I put her under the dryer," she protested.

That was true. I'd watched Lucy mix and apply the dye, per routine. "Did anything happen after that? Like—I don't know—did Margaret ask you for something else to drink or get out of her chair?"

"Not as far as I know." Her eyes welled with tears. "But Sven called right after you left, so I was outside the whole time."

I stood up and walked to her station. "What did you do with the bowl you used to mix the dye?"

"It's in the sink in the break room." She wiped tears from her face. "I haven't washed it or the brush yet."

"Did you use all the dye on her hair?"

She nodded.

I looked again at Lucy's station. The shampoos, conditioners, hair sprays, gels, and other products were lined up neatly in front of the mirror, and the brushes, combs, and hairdryer were in their places. Nothing looked out of the ordinary, and yet something didn't seem right.

* * *

"Don't these people have TVs?" I muttered as I sized up the crowd near the police cars and emergency response vehicles parked in front of The Clip and Sip. Then I threw my head into my lap and wished that the plainclothes detective who had sequestered me had put me anywhere but the front porch. It was the second time in less than five hours that I'd had to endure the concerned and even hostile looks of the townsfolk, and I wasn't sure how much more I could take.

In fact, when Detective Lester Marshall had first introduced himself and led me outside, I seriously considered making a break for it—running as far as I could from the salon and never looking back. But with his dark hair and stocky frame, the detective looked pretty foreboding. Plus, that would have just made me look guilty, especially if Margaret was dead. And at this point I was certain that she was. The emergency medical technicians had been with her since five fifteen, and it was six o'clock. If she'd survived, they would have taken her to the hospital by now.

The salon door burst open, and I bolted upright as Detective Marshall strutted onto the porch with his chest jutting out like a rooster.

"I suppose you know that Margaret Appleby is deceased."

I bowed my head. "I'd gathered as much, yes."

He let out a long, slow breath. "You should count yourself lucky that you were with Detective Ohlsen when she stopped breathing," he began in a dismayed tone, "otherwise, you'd be a prime suspect."

I stared at him, stunned. I couldn't believe that he was talking about suspects so soon after Margaret's passing, and I was shocked by his disappointment that Detective Ohlsen had provided me with an alibi. But I don't know why I was surprised. From the minute Detective Marshall had arrived on the scene, it was clear that he'd been in a hurry to make an arrest.

"As the owner of the old LaSalle brothel," he continued, "you were the first person I was going to question."

I leapt to my feet as anger shot through my veins like rocket fuel. "For your information, this building hasn't been a brothel for over sixty years, and the LaSalle family sold it to my uncle twenty years ago."

"It doesn't matter who owns it. This place is bad news." He gave me a pointed look. "Your uncle found that out the hard way."

I gasped. How could such a clean-cut guy be such a dirty dog?

Detective Marshall pulled out his notepad. "Now, I just questioned your cousin in the break room. She said that there were clients in the salon at the same time as Margaret Appleby. Can you confirm their names?"

"Bertha Braun and Prudence Miller, but—"

"Did anyone else come in?" he interrupted. "Like the mailman…or a supplier? Because I'll need to question them too."

I shook my head and remembered how excited Bertha had been about her date and Prudence her sailing adventure. They'd come in to The Clip and Sip for a pleasant experience, so

I felt awful that they were now involved in this morbid mess. "Why do you have to question them if Margaret died after they left?"

"It's routine procedure to talk to everyone who saw the victim in the hours before death."

"Victim?" I put my hands on my hips. "Aren't you jumping the gun here, Detective? Margaret was eighty years old. Maybe she died of natural causes or a heart condition or something."

"Not a chance," he replied as he straightened his suit coat. "The EMTs said that she was unusually cyanotic—"

"What?" I interrupted (I owed him one). "You can't possibly think we have cyanide in the salon!"

His lips curled. "Cyanosis is when the skin turns blue because of poor circulation or a lack of oxygen in the blood."

"Oh." I collapsed into the swing. "In that case, I agree with the EMTs."

"Sure, sure." He drew his hand to his chin. "But here's the funny part," he said in a voice devoid of humor. "She's been dead for at least an hour, and yet she's still blue."

I thought of the dye but immediately dismissed the notion. "Well, of course. Now that she's dead, she definitely has circulation problems and a lack of oxygen in the blood."

He snorted. "Dead bodies don't turn blue, and they don't *stay* blue either. They turn pink." He stepped closer to the swing. "So, what I want to know is why Margaret is still as blue as the ocean down at the harbor."

My body stiffened as my mind drifted back to the dye. "I'm afraid I can't help you with that."

"That's okay. Because I know someone who can." He looked through the window at Lucy, who was sobbing in a salon chair.

A protective instinct surged through me, and I pounced like a mamma bear. "You can't possibly think that sweet girl would do anything to harm Margaret!"

He shrugged. "She was the last person to see her alive, and from what I understand, she'd just applied blue dye on the victim's hair."

"Exactly," I snapped. "She put it on her *hair*, not in her teacup or anything."

He cocked his head. "Now, that's an interesting remark." A smug smile spread across his lips as he jotted a note on his pad. "Anything else you'd like to add?"

My hand flew to my head, which was again starting to spin—not from an oncoming panic attack but from the absurdity of the situation. *Did Detective Marshall really believe that Margaret had been murdered? Even worse, had I just incriminated Lucy in that poor woman's death?*

Detective Marshall glanced toward the street, and I followed his gaze. One look told me everything I needed to know.

The Crime Scene Response Team had arrived.

* * *

As I contemplated the *3:02 a.m.* reflected on my bedroom ceiling, I regretted buying an alarm clock that projected the time in an eerie blue light. I never wanted to see that color again. Of course, that hadn't stopped me from binging on a half gallon of Tillamook Oregon Blueberry Patch ice cream after the CSR Team had left. But technically, that was purple.

Instead of unplugging the clock, I covered my face with a pillow, halfway hoping that I would suffocate.

Then I heard knocking, and I sat straight up.

The sound was coming from Uncle Vinnie's room next door. *Was it an intruder? Or worse, a killer?*

Fear filled my chest as I crept out of bed and threw on my robe. I opened my door a crack and peered out. The second floor was laid out shotgun-style with three small bedrooms on either side of the hallway and a living room and bathroom at the back of the house. There was a third floor with a walk-in attic and a tower room that my uncle had never gotten around to renovating. Gia and I occupied the two second-floor bedrooms facing the street, so all I had to do was look across the hall to see that her lights were on.

Mustering up my courage, I dashed into her room, wincing at her choice of decor. I'd never taken LSD, but every time I looked at the deep-purple walls, zebra-striped curtains, and fuzzy orange comforter set I felt like I had to be tripping.

Gia sauntered in from the hallway wearing leopard-print footie pajamas with fuchsia angel wings attached to the back and holding a hammer. "Did I wake you up?"

I gritted my teeth. *Nope, not hallucinating*. "You know Vinnie's room is off limits. What were you doing in there?"

"Tapping on the sheetrock and listening for hollow spots." She flopped onto the bed, causing her wings to flap. "I'm positive that he stashed cash in this house. These old brothels were notorious for having hiding places. I read about one that had a system of chutes in the walls so that every hooker had her own specific money drop. How does that saying go? If these old walls could talk…"

"…they'd be charged with public indecency," I concluded as I sunk into a neon-green beanbag chair at the foot of the bed. "And they wouldn't know a thing about any hidden treasure."

"I don't understand why you're so skeptical about the money thing," Gia said as she let the hammer drop to the floor with a thud. "Vinnie left you a paid-off Victorian mansion, not to mention that fine Ferrari we're driving. Seems to me the guy had some cash."

I sighed. "People who have money don't hide it in walls."

"No, they hide it in offshore accounts." She grabbed a pad and pen from her bedside table. "Which is another avenue I need to look into."

"Great, Nancy Drew." I elbowed my way deeper into the chair. "You get right on that."

"I will, because you're going to need some serious dough now that this whole Miss Appleby thing has happened." She jotted down a note and then pointed her pen at me. "And by the way, any lost treasure I find? You're giving me a generous cut."

"If you uncover any wall treasure, I'll gladly split it with you." The accounting quiz I hadn't studied for flashed into my mind. "Because it's looking like I'm never going to get that business degree."

Gia's shoulders slumped. "Don't say that, Cass. Given the circumstances, you can get the professor to give you an extension on your quiz."

"Oh sure," I said, waving my hand, "I'll just tell him that a woman came into my salon, turned blue, and died. Because that's a likely story."

"It's plausible. Just don't mention that she *stayed* blue."

I massaged my temples. "The truth is, I wouldn't pass the quiz even if I did have a few more days to study. Besides, as soon as the news of Margaret's death gets out, I could be too stressed to deal with school."

"Ugh, speaking of the news, I can see the front page of the *Cove Chronicles* now, 'Old Lady Clipped at The Clip and Sip,'" she recited in a dramatic voice. "Or wait. This is better, 'Old Lady Dipped and Clipped at The Clip and Sip.'"

I stared at her, incredulous. "You sound like Detective Marshall! We don't know for sure that Margaret was murdered."

"Are you kidding?" She opened her arms wide. "The woman looked like Cookie Monster, and this ain't *Sesame Street*. That didn't happen by magic."

I sat up in the chair. "Are you implying that Lucy is somehow responsible?"

"That Goody-Two-Shoes?" She straightened a drooping angel wing. "Not a chance."

I bit my thumbnail. "Then that leaves Margaret."

"As in, maybe she was over being old and ended it all by drinking dye?"

I recoiled as though she'd just swung at me with the hammer. "I was thinking more along the lines of she mistook the mixing bowl for her teacup. But now that you mention it, suicide could have been a factor, especially if she had a terminal illness or something."

Gia reached under her bed and pulled out a bag of Tim's Potato Chips. "Either way, it doesn't make sense. If she wanted to off herself, she could've done that at home with a bottle of aspirin. Why go to a salon and drink dye to die?"

I folded my hands in front of my face. "I was wondering the same thing."

"And if she swallowed some dye on accident, she would've spit it back into the bowl. It's no secret that stuff is toxic." She pulled a handful of chips from the bag and then shoved it toward me. "Want some? They're dill pickle flavored."

I wrinkled my nose. "No, but that reminds me. I've heard of elderly people losing their sense of taste. What if she didn't know it was dye?"

"Then why order a soy chai latte and not just plain tea?" Gia popped a chip into her mouth. "If you ask me, the real question is whether Miss Appleby's death had anything to do with Vinnie's murder. I mean, we know those two were connected, if you get what I'm saying."

I got it, all right. My stomach churned at the possibility—and at the pun. "That seems like a stretch, but I'll bet the police look into it. After all, there are two active crime scenes in the house."

Gia chewed another chip. "So, what are you going to do about it?"

"The only thing I can do—wait while the authorities handle it."

"Cassidi!" she exclaimed in a bite-your-tongue tone. "You're half Italian!"

"And?"

"Show some passion!" She sprung to her feet on the bed, producing a flurry of wing flapping, and began punching the air. "Find your fighting spirit!"

I gave her my best blank stare. "To be honest, I've always identified more with my German side."

"Well, stop it, Claudia Schiffer." She punched a fist in my direction. "You can be all logical and practical at school. Right now you have to react."

Gia had a point, albeit an ethnically inappropriate one. Lucy's freedom was at stake, and everything I had was on the line. This wasn't the time to play it safe, particularly when one of the cops on the case was grasping at straws. I had to do my part to prove Lucy's innocence, protect my home, and save the salon. With any luck, I'd resuscitate the Conti reputation in the process. "You're right. I need to do something."

"OMG! You're admitting that I'm right?" She held up her arms and fell backward onto the bed. "Have I died and gone to heaven?"

I smirked. "Don't get carried away—by those wings of yours."

She hopped up and sat cross-legged on the bed. "So, what's the plan? Are you going to be like Jessica Fletcher and go around Danger Cove investigating people?"

I shifted in my seat. "I hadn't really thought about it. But if I did, I'd like to be someone younger, like Veronica Mars."

"Well, whoever you are, you can totally count on me to be your sleuthing sidekick—you know I never miss an episode of *48 Hours*. And Amy could help with library research. With three brilliant criminal minds like ours on the case, it'll be a piece of cake," she said with a snap of her fingers.

Criminal minds? Okay, so I had my doubts about Gia's abilities, but Amy was a genius. She could probably solve this case with her brain waves alone.

"And who knows?" she continued. "Maybe we could solve Vinnie's murder too."

I stared at her, surprised. It had never occurred to me to look into my uncle's death—I guess because I'd just assumed that the police would have solved the mystery of his murder by now. "Sure," I said, although I was anything but. "Now, if I'm going to sleuth, I've got to sleep." I rolled from the chair. "No more hammering, okay?"

She gave the thumbs-up sign. "You got it, *cug*," she said, using an abbreviation of the Italian word *cugina*, or "cousin," which everyone always thought was short for *Cujo*.

No sooner had I crossed the hallway than my resolve waned. As I climbed into bed, I wondered what I was getting myself into. I was already trying to get established in a new town, run a salon, and earn a business degree, and I was failing at all three. Plus, the closest I'd ever come to detective work was when I tracked down a missing skirt at the drycleaners. So, investigating a suspicious death seemed more than a little outside my area of expertise.

And what if Margaret *had* been murdered like my uncle? And what if their deaths were related?

I shivered and pulled the covers up to my chin.

Uh-uh. I couldn't go around town questioning people and poking into their private lives. I was no Jessica Fletcher or Veronica Mars. I was Cassidi Lee Conti, a hairstylist from Fredericksburg, Texas. And regardless of what happened in those cozy mysteries, I knew that real-life hairstylists didn't go around investigating murders. No, I was going to do the smart thing and leave Margaret's case in the hands of the qualified professionals.

I turned to my side and closed my eyes, but I couldn't sleep. Something was eating at my gut, and it wasn't fear—or that Oregon Blueberry Patch ice cream. It was guilt. My Uncle Vinnie had shocked our entire family by leaving all his worldly possessions to me. He'd explained his decision in his will, stating that I was the only member of the family who would give The Yankee Clipper, as he had called the salon, "the love the old girl needed." (In retrospect, I wish he'd used a different phrase, but whatever.) He'd believed in me, so I had to repay his trust, not to mention his generosity. To do that, I not only had to save The Clip and Sip, but I had to find his killer too—whether his death was connected to Margaret's or not.

I rolled onto my back and covered my face with a pillow.

If I made it through what was left of this wretched night, I would start my inquiry after breakfast.

And I knew exactly who to investigate first.

CHAPTER FOUR

"Here's your espresso," the baby-faced teen said as he placed the cup and saucer on the weathered table outside Carolyn's Coffee and Creamery.

I flashed a wan smile and dumped three packets of sugar into the black gold. It was only 7:00 a.m., and I was in no mood for anything bitter.

As I stirred the sweetener, a breeze blew across the pier, and the combined aroma of the sea air and the coffee soothed my nerves. A small seagull perched on the pier railing caught my eye, and I felt an unexpected moment of calm.

A thwack shattered my serenity as a copy of the *Cove Chronicles* landed beside my cup.

"If you haven't seen this morning's paper, you'd better take a look," Amy warned. She was standing before me in a stark gray sack dress, and her mouth was set in a grim line. "And prepare yourself," she continued as she dropped into a chair. "It's pure yellow journalism."

Better than blue journalism. Or so I thought. When I opened the paper, a photograph of spread-eagle Sadie with the caption "Sex and Suffocation at the Salon?" greeted me.

Without a word, I tossed back my espresso like it was a shot of whiskey. Gia's titles suddenly sounded a lot more appealing.

The young server approached and took my cup. "Can I get you anything else, ma'am?"

"I'll have another," I whispered, too shocked to be upset about that "ma'am." "And make it a double."

"Whoa." Amy raised her hand in a stopping motion. "Pull the reigns on the caffeine, cowgirl. My mother says it's like rock music—it causes addictions to cigarettes and reefers."

Amy, like her mother, obviously, was more than a little square. "First of all, I might be from Texas, but I'm no cowgirl. And second, if anything's going to drive me to drugs, it's stories about people suffocating in my salon, not a few shots of espresso in my system."

Her eyes grew wide. "Be careful, then, Cass. Because the reporter who wrote that article is convinced that there was some sort of funny business going on at The Clip and Sip."

I sighed—both because of the reporter's cheekiness and because of Amy's cluelessness. For such a bright girl, she often struggled with the difference between sarcasm and seriousness. "Who is this reporter, anyway?"

"Duncan Pickles. And the surname fits him. He's a real *sauertopf*."

I gave a frustrated sigh. Amy was German on her father's side, but she told me that she hadn't known a word of the language until she'd studied it in college. Since that time, she'd taken to peppering her speech with the occasional Deutsch word "to exercise her ancestral right to speak the 'fatherland tongue.'" "You know, just because I'm half German and grew up in a town settled by German immigrants doesn't mean I can understand the language."

"But it's so close to English," she whined.

"Maybe to you, but it's Greek to me."

"No." She shook her head. "It's German."

I rolled my eyes. "Would you just tell me what a *sauertopf* is?"

"A 'sour pot.'"

I could think of other things I'd like to call that reporter. "So, I assume that he was the camera-wielding blond I saw standing in the crowd?"

"Yeah." She flashed a goofy grin. "He's a real sex pot, isn't he? But his camera is the least of your concerns. Wait until you read what he wrote in the article."

Against my better judgment, I picked up the paper.

Amy tapped the page from behind. "Read it aloud. I want to hear it."

I put the paper down and stared at her long and hard. Then I began to read in a low voice. "'Almost a year after the salacious murder of salon owner and Cove Casanova Vincent Conti...'"

"Cove Casanova?" I exclaimed, outraged. "Where does he get off talking about my uncle like that?"

She pursed her lips. "That part is actually true."

I glared at her and resumed reading. "'...the specter of sex and death still looms large over The Clip and Sip. Literally. Within hours of a tasteless, not to mention dangerous, publicity stunt involving a lewd statue suspended from a pulley...'"

I gasped. "He thinks that I had Sadie out there swinging her stuff as a publicity stunt?"

"Well, her stuff did draw a sizeable crowd."

I gave her a half-lidded stare and then continued reading. "'...long-time Danger Cove resident Margaret Appleby was found unresponsive under a hair dryer following a routine touch up to her blue hair dye. Attempts to revive her were unsuccessful."

"Duncan did you a favor there," Amy said. "He could have mentioned that she was abnormally blue."

I leaned across the table. "Whose side are you on here?"

She put her hand on her chest. "Yours. But when you break the story down like that, you can see how he came up with the version that he did."

"All I can see is that he twisted the facts to write a sensational story." I pushed the paper away. "I refuse to read another word."

"But you haven't gotten to the best part." Amy grabbed the paper and began to read—with gusto. "'Although police haven't released any information about the incident, there is reason to suspect foul play. Medics at the scene initially believed that the deceased was deprived of oxygen. But an EMT was overheard stating that hours after her demise, she was 'still bluer than a bluefish swimming in Ty-D-Bol,' which begs the question—Did Margaret Appleby die from dye?'"

I clenched my jaw. "She wasn't *that* blue."

"I'd say any amount of blue is pretty darn blue," Amy said as she folded the paper.

The server deposited my double espresso on the table, and I reached for eight packets of sugar. Despite my efforts, this day was getting more bitter by the minute.

"Listen," I began, "I didn't ask you to meet me because I wanted to discuss the details of the incident, okay? The truth is—I need your help with some research."

Amy's face lit up. "For your accounting class?"

"I've got that covered," I replied, neglecting to mention that I'd picked *C* for every answer on the online multiple-choice quiz before coming to meet her. "What I need to know is whether swallowing blue hair dye can cause a person's body to turn blue."

Her face darkened. "You're not thinking about interfering in the police investigation, are you?"

"Of course not. But after my encounter with Detective Marshall last night, I decided to do some asking around—you know, to see what I can find out."

"Are you sure that's a good idea? If this does turn out to be a murder, you could be a target yourself, for all we know."

This time I chugged my double espresso. I hadn't even considered the possibility that I could be next on some crazed killer's list. But why would anyone want to kill me? Was there some twisted plot to kill off the Contis, and Margaret somehow got in the way?

The little seagull hopped into my line of vision. Then it swooped down and plucked a fish from the water. I shuddered. *Was that some kind of sign?*

"Are you cold?" Amy asked. "I've got an extra sweater in my satchel."

I shook my head and tried to recoup the courage I'd gathered the night before. "You know, if there is someone out to get me, then that's even more of a reason to look into what happened to Margaret. Besides, Gia said she would help."

She lurched forward as her elbow fell off the table. "You want your *cousin* to help you?"

Amy and Gia were like oil and water, or maybe I should say like beer and Chianti. "Gia's a little over the top, but I'll give her this—she's *über* resourceful," I replied, using an adjective that Amy would understand. "Right now, for instance, because of all the money problems we're having, she's hunting for some cash my uncle supposedly hid. She calls it his 'lost treasure.'"

"I didn't take you for a treasure hunter," a male voice said.

I turned and saw Zac holding a to-go coffee.

"I was talking about my cousin." I crossed my arms, annoyed that he'd eavesdropped on our conversation. I looked at Amy to see whether she was irritated too. Quite the contrary. Her face was flushed, and she was batting her eyelashes at the speed of a hummingbird flapping its wings.

"Well, if she's looking for treasure, she's come to the right place." He gestured toward the water. "A British ship called *Ocean's Revenge* sunk out there somewhere in 1852, and the booty that the pirate Bart Coffyn looted from Sir Francis Drake in 1579 is rumored to be buried here too."

"Well, aren't you the maritime history buff," Amy exclaimed, drawing out the word "buff" as she gawked at his biceps.

Zac grinned. "It was my father's passion."

"We have a large collection of books on local piracy at the library." Amy twirled a lock of mousy brown hair around her finger. "If you'd like to stop by sometime, I'd be happy to help you deepen your knowledge of the subject."

Oh, brother. I cleared my throat. "If you don't mind, Zac, we were in the middle of a private conversation."

The smile faded from his lips. "Sure, I need to get to work anyway. I just stopped to tell you how sorry I was to hear about what happened at your salon yesterday."

My stomach fell like a suspended statue cut from a rope. "I'm sorry. I didn't realize you knew."

"Margaret Appleby was an acquaintance of my grandma's."

Now he had my undivided attention. "Did your grandmother know her well?"

"Not really. They quilted together a few times after Margaret had to quit the Danger Cove Quilt Guild."

Amy attempted a sexy stare over the thick black rim of her glasses. "You know about quilting too? A man after my own heart."

I kicked her under the table. "Um, Zac," I began as I caught a glimpse of Amy pointing toward the ground and mouthing "ow," "why did Margaret have to quit the guild?"

He swallowed a sip of coffee. "I'm not sure exactly. But this morning I stopped by my mom's house, and I heard my grandma telling her that it had something to do with a woman named Bertha Braun."

My heart started racing, but I played it cool. I couldn't let Zac know that I was investigating Margaret's death. Word spread like wildfire in Danger Cove. "Do you think your grandmother would be willing to talk to me about Margaret?"

He shrugged. "Honestly, I think the best person to talk to would be the woman who runs the guild."

"Dee Madison," Amy interjected. "She and her best friend, Emma Quinn, come into the library to check out quilting books. They're quite fascinating—the books, I mean."

Yeah, as interesting as the history of the needle and thread. "I'll do that, Zac. And thanks."

He looked me in the eyes. "Promise you'll let me know if there's anything else I can do?"

I looked away. Even though I'd sworn off the color blue for the rest of my life, there was something about the shade of his eyes that almost made me want to change my mind. "Definitely."

As he walked in the direction of the Pirate's Hook Marine Services, I pushed back my chair before Amy could punch me in the arm or return my kick. "So, where do I find this Dee person?"

She rose to her feet. "The Danger Cove Historical Museum. The guild has been holed up there for the past couple of days trying to finish some quilts for the lighthouse fundraiser tonight," she said as she walked over to the bike rack. "If you want to ride on the handlebars, I could drop you off on my way to work."

"I'd rather walk." I removed eight dollars from my wallet and placed it under the sugar caddy. "It'll give me time to think about what I should ask Dee."

"Suit yourself." Amy mounted her bicycle. "But be careful how you approach her. She's a real handful."

As I headed up the pier toward Main Street, I thought about Amy's warning. I wasn't sure how I was going to handle Dee or this whole situation. I mean, back home I wasn't exactly known as "the girl most likely to dig in her heels" when the going got rough. I was more like "the girl most likely to hike up her skirt and run." The most infamous example was when I broke off my engagement to Shane—at the altar. Yes, I was a runaway bride, but not because of my anxiety issue, because that actually started happening after I ran. It was because I realized a little late in the game that my impending marriage was a knee-jerk reaction to my parents' divorce.

But this was the new, do-over me. And if I could handle the likes of Gia and Amy, I could handle anyone.

Except for maybe Bertha Braun.

* * *

My thighs burned as I climbed the never-ending concrete staircase to the second floor of the Danger Cove Historical Museum. I resolved to find a gym with a StairMaster or do some hiking around the cove, but only after this whole mess at the salon was behind me, of course.

When I finally reached the landing, I headed down the hallway to the community room and peered inside. Except for the high ceilings and the large windows overlooking Main Street, the space looked something like a clothing sweatshop. It was arranged in an assembly line for various stages of the quilt-making process. Everywhere I looked, women were hard at work cutting, basting, sewing, and ironing. There were even a few men helping out, and an adorable labradoodle service dog was curled up on the floor.

"Aren't you the Conti girl?" a frail-looking, white-haired woman asked. She was seated at a table near the door, hand sewing binding to the back of a quilt.

"Yes, ma'am." I was tempted to clarify that my name was Cassidi, but I thought better of it. Judging from her gruff tone, the woman was nowhere near as docile as she looked.

"Nasty business at The Clip and Sip yesterday," she said, keeping her eyes focused on her stitching.

I opened my mouth to reply, but the word "nasty" threw me. I wasn't sure whether she was talking about what had happened with Margaret or with Sadie and Pearl.

"Don't just stand there, dear," a tall woman in her mid-sixties said as she approached with a spool of white thread. "Come in."

I stepped inside but stayed close to the door. Something about the white-haired one made me uneasy.

"I'm Emma Quinn, and this is my friend Dee Madison," she said, gesturing toward the older woman. "Are you a quilter, Cassidi?"

I blinked. I don't know why, but it still surprised me when townspeople knew my name. "Uh, no, ma'am. My mother and my grandmother quilt, but I don't sew."

She smiled and smoothed her dyed brown hair. "Well, if you'd like to learn, you've come to the right place. The people in this room have hundreds of years of combined experience, and Dee used to be a quilting teacher."

"Actually," I began, turning to face Dee, "I came to talk to Ms. Madison about Margaret Appleby."

Emma exchanged a look with Dee as she placed the spool in front of her.

"Have a seat," Dee said, her gaze still fixed on the quilt. "Whatever you have to say to me, you can say to Emma. She knew Margaret too."

I sat at the end of the table and angled a glance at Dee. From what I could tell, she was around the same age as Margaret. "How long did the two of you know Margaret?"

"About five years, I'd say," Emma replied as she removed several pins from a pincushion.

Dee jabbed her needle into the quilt. "I met her when she moved to Danger Cove some thirty years ago."

I leaned forward in my chair. "Wow, so you must have been pretty close."

"Can't say we were," Dee replied. "Margaret kept to herself."

"That's weird." I looked down at colorful strips of fabric that had been sewn together into binding. "Whenever she was at the salon, she was always chatting about her friends around town."

Emma stood over the table and began pinning a strip of binding to the edge of a sampler quilt. "What Dee means is that Margaret was private. Unlike the rest of us, she didn't talk about herself or her family at meetings."

Now that she mentioned it, I realized that I'd never heard Margaret share anything personal when she came into the salon—that is, apart from the jaw-dropper about her and my uncle. "But was Margaret still a guild member? I heard that she had to quit because of some sort of issue with Bertha Braun."

Dee grunted and grabbed a pair of scissors, and I scooted my chair back a few inches—just in case. "Bertha's the one we asked to leave. But Margaret quit around that same time because of her rheumatoid arthritis."

I nodded, remembering Margaret's deformed fingers on my arm.

"Margaret and Bertha butted heads like two bighorn sheep from the day they met," Dee continued as she clipped a few stray threads from the quilt.

Emma stood up and massaged her lower back. "Those two didn't see eye to eye on anything."

"I noticed," I said. "At the salon yesterday, things got ugly when Ms. Braun started bragging to Margaret about an upcoming date with some man."

Dee arched a white brow. "With Santiago Beltrán, I presume."

"How'd you know?" I asked.

Emma waved her hand in a shooing motion. "Oh, they'd been fighting over him for ages, the ninnies."

Dee gave me a steely stare. "Like your Uncle Vincent, Santiago's something of a local Lothario—but among the older crowd. He lives at the Coveside Retirement Resort."

My cheeks grew hot from embarrassment. If Margaret was any indication, Uncle Vinnie had been popular with the elderly ladies too. But I kept that little tidbit to myself. "Did Santiago have anything to do with Margaret leaving the guild?"

Emma removed a pin from between her lips and inserted it into the binding. "Indirectly. Bertha found out that Margaret was making him a quilt, and she pitched a fit."

"That's putting it mildly," Dee remarked. "What she said was that if Margaret so much as mailed him that quilt, she'd kill her."

I flinched as though I were the one who'd been threatened. "Are you sure she used the word *kill*?"

"Not only that," Emma began, "she said that she was going to skin her like Buffalo Bill did to those women in *Silence of the Lambs*."

My jaw fell open, and I gripped the edges of my seat. "*Skin* her?"

"And make a quilt out of her," Dee added in a matter-of-fact tone.

Emma nodded. "Yes, because remember that Buffalo Bill was going to make a woman suit from the flesh of his victims."

I was speechless. Bertha was a bully, but I never dreamed she would make such a violent threat to anyone.

Dee snipped her sewing thread. "And old Bulldog could have done it too. Before she retired, she was a surgical nurse for Dr. Seth Windom, our resident orthopedist."

"But she didn't do it, Dee." Emma turned to me. "Surely you don't think Bertha had anything to do with Margaret's death? The paper suggested that she was poisoned with hair dye. How else would she turn as blue as Tide liquid detergent?"

"Not Tide," Dee barked. "Ty-D-Bol."

Emma pressed a hand to her forehead. "Oh, that's right."

Dee tossed the scissors on the table, and the clatter practically made me jump out of my skin—er, let's leave it at "jump." "Have you questioned that hairdresser of yours, Lucy O'Connell? After all, she was alone with Margaret while you and your step-cousin were out."

I looked at her open-mouthed. Was there anything this woman didn't know? "Honestly, Lucy is the last person I would suspect of something so terrible."

"Well then, you might want to keep this in mind," Dee began, pointing her needle at me. "You never really know people, not even the ones you're close to."

I leaned back a little, not so much from surprise but to get away from that needle. Dee had a point though. I'd misread Margaret Appleby, and I'd definitely underestimated my uncle. "I'll think about that, Ms. Madison. Now, I'd better get back to the salon. Thank you both for your time."

"You're welcome, dear," Emma said. "And if you ever want to take up quilting, you let us know."

I smiled and fled the room. I don't know what I wanted to escape more—Dee's seeming omniscience or the thought of learning to quilt with her.

Still, as I hurried down the stairs, Dee's last remark echoed through my mind. I just assumed that people around me were good, even if some of them were a little rough around the edges. But what did I really know about Bertha? Sure, she was notorious around town for her bad attitude. And she'd threatened Margaret twice, once really graphically. The question was, did that mean she'd murdered Margaret? And if so, how in the world had she done it?

CHAPTER FIVE

A cold wind blew as I walked up Fletcher Way toward the salon. I pulled my scarf tighter around my neck and glanced at the sky. Black storm clouds were rolling in like harbingers of bad news.

"Super," I muttered as I quickened my pace and glanced at my watch. It was almost nine o'clock, which was when the salon normally opened. But not today. The police had asked that I leave the crime scene untouched until Saturday, and naturally, I obliged. It wasn't like we were going to lose any business.

My "Whip My Hair" ringtone sounded. I pulled my phone from my Kate Spade shoulder bag and saw Amy Spannagel on the display. I pressed Answer. "Hey. What'd you find out about the dye?"

"I have to make this quick," she whispered. "If Ben catches me making a personal call, he'll dock my pay again."

Head Librarian Ben Bardsley was the only person in Danger Cove who was more tight-fisted than Amy. "So, this has happened before?"

"Yeah, I was thirty seconds late coming back from your place after lunch yesterday. And this morning he's been threatening to charge me for sharpening the pencils."

"Wait. Aren't they supposed to be sharpened?"

"Of course," she replied as though I were the dullest pencil in the box. "But he claims that I sharpen them too often. Scout's honor though, Cass, I wait until the points are dull. I'm no lead waster."

I didn't doubt it for a second. Amy was the thriftiest person I knew, not to mention the only woman in Washington State who'd been a Boy Scout—until the organization found out she was a girl, that is. She sewed her own clothes and grew her own food. She even made her own kitchen knives.

"Anyway," she continued, "I couldn't find any scientific studies indicating that the ingestion of hair dye alters skin color, but that doesn't mean it couldn't happen. I did learn that swallowing hair dye can cause rashes, edema, puss-filled blisters, oozing lesions—"

My stomach began to churn. "Wow, we've been talking for almost a whole minute now," I interrupted. "You'd better get back to work."

"*Meine Güte*," she exclaimed. "See you at your place at five."

I hung up, wondering why Amy couldn't just say "my goodness" like other people and wishing that I didn't have to go out. But the Smugglers' Tavern was hosting a fundraiser for the Danger Cove Lighthouse, and as a local business owner, I was obligated to make an appearance—and a donation, which I didn't have. Plus, my absence could be interpreted as an indirect admission that the salon was culpable in Margaret's death, and I couldn't let that happen.

As I crossed the lawn of The Clip and Sip, a breeze blew a Styrofoam cup from the porch. Thanks to the activity from last night, the grass was trampled, and litter was scattered across the property. Extracting a tissue from my purse, I bent down to retrieve the cup, some paper, and several cigarette butts. Then I headed around the left side of the building, and I removed a piece of plastic from the flower garden. It was a syringe wrapper, which I hoped had come from the EMTs. The last thing I needed on top of everything else was people shooting up at the salon.

I unlocked the back door and stuffed the items into the overflowing trash bin. As usual, Gia had neglected to empty it into the Dumpster in the parking lot out back. I sighed and headed for the stairs.

Glass shattered in the salon.

I stopped cold. Was that the killer returning for some sort of evidence? Or had I been watching too many reruns of *Murder, She Wrote*? To be on the safe side, I crept toward the back door.

The sound of a woman's sobs filled the break room.

Killers don't cry. I turned and peered into the salon.

Lucy was standing at her station, staring at a broken picture frame on the ground. "It's a sign, isn't it?"

"What?" I asked as I rushed to her side.

She squatted and brushed shards of glass from the picture. "Sven and I had this made the day he proposed."

"Oh, Lucy," I said, crouching beside her. "Everything is going to be okay."

"I'm scared, Cassidi." A tear rolled down her cheek. "I can tell that the police think I had something to do with Margaret's death."

"Well, you're innocent." I put my hand on her arm. "I'm going to help you prove that."

Her eyes lit up, but then she frowned and looked at the picture. "There's something you should know."

The back door slammed, and Gia clomped into the room in combat boots, a red spandex crop top, and low-rise camouflage pants.

I couldn't tell whether she was trying to blend in or stand out. "That's a lot of belly you're baring, soldier."

"Never mind me, wise guy." She crossed her arms. "Why are you two doing squats in the middle of the crime scene?"

I rose to my feet. "Um, obviously we're not working out. Lucy dropped her engagement photo."

"*Marone*," Gia exclaimed, using the Jersey variant of "Madonna." She pointed at Lucy. "You've got the *maliocch'*."

I shot her a shut-your-mouth look. "There's no such thing as the 'evil eye.'"

"Even you can't deny that bad things are happening to her, Cassidi."

"She's right," Lucy said. "I'm supposed to be getting married, but instead I could be going to prison."

Gia snorted. "If that's all you're worried about, then I have some good news for you—marriage and prison are the same thing."

I put my hand on Gia's back and pushed her toward the break room. "Why don't you go make Lucy a nice cup of chamomile tea?"

"If you ask me," she grumbled, "what the girl needs is a shot of lime vodka."

In Gia's world, there was an appropriate flavor of vodka for every occasion. "Well, I didn't ask you."

She flipped her hair and marched into the break room.

I turned toward Lucy. "What did you want to tell me?"

"It was nothing," she said, grabbing a broom.

I gestured toward the broken frame. "Leave that. We shouldn't do any sweeping without police permission."

"Okay." She leaned the broom against the wall. "You know, I think I'm going to go home and lie down."

"That's a good idea. Do you still want to come to the fundraiser tonight? It may do you good to get out."

"Maybe," she said, running a hand through her red locks. "I'll see how I feel later."

I gave her a hug. "Try not to worry."

She nodded and headed for the break room.

I turned and stared at Lucy's station. I hated to see her so scared, but I couldn't blame her. I was scared too, and I had an airtight alibi. Still, I couldn't help but think about what Dee had said. Truth be told, I didn't know Lucy all that well. And it seemed like she'd wanted to confess something to me before. But what?

Gia stomped into the salon. "Who's gonna drink that tea I'm making?"

"I will." With her around, I could use a calming beverage. "I wish you hadn't come in when you did. Lucy was about to tell me something important."

She rolled her eyes. "What? The Swedish meatball said he'd still marry her if she went to jail?"

"His name is Sven Mattsun," I replied. "And it wasn't about him."

Her eyes narrowed. "Do you think it had something to do with Miss Appleby?"

"I think so, but I can't imagine what."

Gia slipped her hands into her front pockets. "Actually, I've been thinking about something she said last night when she called 9-1-1."

"What?" I asked as I again surveyed the contents of Lucy's counter.

"Don't you think it's kind of weird that she told the 9-1-1 operator that there'd been 'an accident'?"

At the time, I hadn't paid much attention to what Lucy was saying. But now that Gia mentioned it, "accident" did seem like an odd word to use. "She was probably just guessing about what had happened. I mean, none of us could've anticipated a possible murder."

"But if I were guessing, I would've said that Miss Appleby had stopped breathing. After all, she was as old as Methuselah and as blue as a bottle of blue Curaçao."

The teapot began to whistle, to my relief.

"That thing's obnoxious," Gia exclaimed as she tramped into the break room.

I put my hands on my hips and thought about how I had to yell at Lucy to get her to realize that Margaret was blue. Clearly, she'd been too shocked to process everything that was happening.

But how *did* Margaret turn blue?

I stood behind Lucy's salon chair and mentally retraced her steps. She said that she'd used all the dye on Margaret's hair before putting her under the dryer. Then she must've taken the bowl and brush to the sink on her way outside to talk to Sven, because they weren't at her station when she came running back inside. So, if Margaret had swallowed dye, it would have had to happen after Lucy went out back. But that wasn't possible, because we didn't have any more blue dye in the salon.

The only other possibility I could think of was that the killer had brought dye into the salon and forced Margaret to drink it while Lucy was outside. Since she was arguing with Sven, she wouldn't have heard the commotion.

But why *blue* dye? Was it simply to frame Lucy? Or was there some significance to the color?

"Your Majesty," Gia announced as she placed a teacup and saucer on Lucy's station.

That's when I noticed it, and a piece of the puzzle fell into place.

"I have a doctor's appointment to get to," I said, hurrying toward the break room. "I'll be back in time to get ready for the lighthouse fundraiser."

"What about the tea?" she called.

"You drink it." I grabbed my bag from the table. "It works wonders for sallow skin."

"*Disgraziade*!" she yelled as I ran out the door.

I smiled at the "disgrace" insult and tapped a number on my phone before jumping into the Ferrari, which, incidentally, is a pretty awesome feeling. The call went straight to voice mail. "Amy, forget the hair dye," I gushed as I started the engine. "I need you to find everything you can on Barbicide."

* * *

The exam room door opened, and a heavyset male with snow-white hair entered holding a file. "Hello. I'm Dr. Windom."

"Thanks for working me in to see you today," I said, pulling the patient gown over my thighs.

"Don't thank me. Thank my receptionist," he said thoughtfully as he took a seat on a stool and began to scan my patient intake forms.

From what I could tell, Seth Windom was in his late seventies, if not even older, so I was kind of surprised that he was still practicing medicine.

"The problem is your left knee, correct?"

"Mm-hm," I replied with a twinge of guilt. It was true that I had a trick knee, but at the moment, this was just the trick part without the knee.

"All right, then," he began, tossing my file onto the counter. "Let's take a look." He rolled his stool to the examining table and pressed the fleshy areas around my knee.

I estimated that I had about two minutes before he realized that I wasn't injured, but I couldn't figure out how to bring up Bertha.

"No sign of swelling," he observed as he reached for a rubber hammer. "Let's test your reflexes."

He tapped my knee, and my foot kicked forward like a traitor.

Dr. Windom placed his hands on his thighs and pursed his lips. "I don't see any indication of a dislocation or a sprain. What were you doing when you reinjured it?"

This was my chance. "Well, as you may have read in the paper this morning, something awful happened at my salon last night. We found one of our clients, Margaret Appleby, unconscious, and I tweaked my knee trying to administer aid."

He nodded and looked down. "She was a longtime patient of mine. I just saw her a few weeks ago."

Now this was news. If Margaret was seeing an orthopedist, maybe she *had* been ill. But I had to find out whether it was terminal. "The whole thing was such a shock," I said. "I mean, she seemed to be in excellent health for a woman her age."

"It is a shame." He checked a box on my diagnosis form. "I'd expected her to make it to a hundred."

Bingo. If Dr. Windom thought she was good for another twenty years, then I could probably rule out an illness-related suicide.

"Speaking of health," he began, looking at me over his bifocals, "I think you're just experiencing some normal aches and pains. But if you'd like, I could have one of my technicians x-ray your ACL."

I wasn't sure whether my insurance would cover the full cost of an X-ray, but I needed to buy more time. "That would be great."

"Fine. Just give me a minute to write up the order."

While he filled out the paperwork, I looked at the pale-blue of my gown and thought of Margaret. "You know, I'm kind of surprised that Margaret was a patient here."

"Oh? Why's that?" he asked without looking up from the forms.

"Well, I heard that Bertha Braun used to work for you and that Margaret and Bertha were in a pretty nasty feud."

"Is that right," he said in a distracted tone.

"Yeah. Apparently, Bertha threatened her." I paused for effect. "More than once."

He put his pen down and removed his glasses. "If I didn't know better, young lady, I'd say you were trying to pump me for information."

I was so embarrassed that I stopped breathing.

Dr. Windom rose to his feet and tucked his glasses inside the pocket of his lab coat. "You'll have to go back into the waiting room, so you'll need to change into your street clothes. A nurse will call you for the X-ray."

"Thanks," I said, still half holding my breath.

He stared at me for a moment and then left the room.

I let out a long exhale. If he'd waited any longer, I would have turned as blue as Margaret. Well, not *that* blue. But clearly, I wasn't going to get any more information from Dr. Windom. I just hoped that the X-ray tech would be more forthcoming.

I hopped from the examining table and pulled on my clothes. When I returned to the lobby, I froze. There was only one available seat, and it was right next to that gossip Donna Bocca. I grabbed a magazine and held it up as though I were reading it as I sat down.

"Look who's trying not to show her face around town," Donna needled. "Tell me—are you here because you hurt yourself watching Zac Taylor manhandle those sex statues? Or did it happen when you doused Margaret Appleby with a fatal dose of hair dye?"

I kept my gaze glued to the magazine and said nothing.

"Just can't tear yourself away from *Orthopedics Today*, can you?"

I dropped the magazine and turned to face her. I wanted to dislike Donna, but I couldn't. She reminded me of a cross between Pumbaa from *The Lion King* and my Italian great-aunts on my father's side—a wide nose, a stubby body, and a mustache. "For your information, I never touched Margaret."

"Then it had to be one of your hairdressers. Which one was it? That flighty O'Connell girl? Or that crazy cousin of yours?"

I threw the magazine onto the table. "That's none of your business. Besides, Margaret could've died of natural causes, you know."

Donna smirked, causing her mustache to fluff. "Not when she turned as blue as a bottle of NyQuil, she didn't."

I sighed. The blue analogies were getting blooming annoying. "Look, even if someone did do something to harm Margaret, why do you think that it was one of us? Her stylist wasn't with her every second, and there were other people in the salon that day."

"Really?" Her eyes lit up like a slot machine that had just hit the jackpot, and she scooted her chair closer to mine. "Like who, for instance?"

I leaned back. Donna smelled like Pumbaa and my paternal aunts too—kind of a cross between musk and garlic. "I couldn't tell you that even if I wanted to." I gave her a pointed look and added, "And as I'm sure you already know, the police are investigating what happened. So, let them do their job, okay?"

"Well," Donna exclaimed, her oversized nostrils flaring. She crossed her arms and turned away.

The main door to the office opened, and a haggard-looking, fifty-something male with his arm in a sling entered and approached the reception desk. He handed a stack of paperwork to the middle-aged brunette behind the glass partition. "I'm Clyde Willard," he said in a gravelly voice. "I have a two o'clock appointment."

"This is a workers' compensation case, right?" she asked as she flipped through the papers.

"Yeah, a couple of us was in an accident out at the Pirate's Hook Marine Services," he replied in a thick southern accent. "A boat we was workin' on came off its stilts, and I fell and busted up my arm."

"I'm sorry to hear that, Mr. Willard," the receptionist replied.

I thought about Zac and wondered whether he'd been injured too. Not that it mattered to me on a personal level, of course. It's just that I hated to see anyone get hurt.

The receptionist handed Clyde a clipboard. "Fill this out, and a nurse will call you back in a few minutes."

He took the clipboard with his free hand. "Is Bertha around?"

My ears pricked up. From the sound of things, Bulldog knew every man in town.

"She hasn't worked here for over a year."

He nodded and took a vacated seat.

Donna leaned toward me. "It's a good thing for us that Bertha's gone."

I looked at her, confused. Apparently, her outrage of moments before was overcome by her need to gossip. "What do you mean?"

She looked from side to side to make sure that no one was listening. "Bertha worked for Dr. Windom for years. She did everything from suture patients after surgery to prescribing their pain meds."

"But she's retired now, right?"

Donna shot me a knowing look and clasped her hands around her crossed leg. "Yes, but she was forced into retirement." She gave a smug smile. "As in, f-i-r-e-d."

"Fired?" I straightened in my seat. "How do you know that?"

She held her nose high. "I'd rather not name names, because I'm not one to gossip, you know. But I'm friends with Dr. Windom's previous receptionist, and she was here when he let Bertha go." She glanced around the room and leaned in. "A former patient had filed a complaint against Bertha."

"Do you know why?" I whispered.

She leaned back and put a hand on her hip. "Does the pope know he's Catholic?" Then she shielded her mouth with her hand. "After a routine surgery, Bertha prescribed the pain reliever Darvocet to the patient, knowing full well that she was violently allergic to it. The woman got so sick," she began, her eyes opening wide, "*it was coming out both ends*."

I was shocked, not to mention disgusted. I mean, I could have done without that last detail. "Did the woman press charges?"

Donna shook her head. "She couldn't."

"Why not? Was there no evidence?"

"That, and..." Her voice trailed off, and she gave a wry smile as she savored the suspense she was creating. "...she died."

I gasped and put my hand to my chest. "From the Darvocet?"

"That would've made for a much better story, wouldn't it?" She gave a disappointed sigh. "But she died from complications following the surgery. Dr. Windom reported the Darvocet incident to the police, though. He knew that the allergy had been documented in the patient's file and that Bertha must've deleted it."

"Maybe it was deleted by accident," I suggested. "If you press the wrong computer key, you can lose an entire document."

"Who said anything about computers?" Donna asked. "According to my friend, Dr. Windom only made the switch to electronic medical records after the incident with Bertha. So the patient's file was the old-school paper version, and someone had clearly used Wite-Out to delete Darvocet from her list of drug allergies."

My eyes widened in surprise.

"Unfortunately," she continued, "nothing ever came of it. That sort of thing is hard to prove."

"Did anyone ever find out why Bertha did it?"

"This is where it gets good," Donna replied, giving my arm a shove. "It was the old green-eyed monster. Bertha had found out that the woman was flirting with a man she'd been seeing."

My heart started pounding so hard that I could barely breathe. All I could spit out was, "Who?"

She shrugged. "Some older gentleman who passed away a few years back. But does it matter?"

No, it didn't. Because I already knew everything I needed to know.

Bertha Braun had worked in healthcare for a long time, so she would have known about the toxicity of Barbicide. More importantly, she had a history of poisoning her romantic rivals.

CHAPTER SIX

Gia skidded the Ferrari to a stop in front of Amy's gingerbread-style house at five o'clock on the dot and laid on the horn. "Looks like something straight out of friggin' 'Hansel and Gretel.'"

"I know," I said, regretting my decision to cave in to Gia's request to drive. "Every time I come here, I halfway expect a witch to come out."

"Yeah. Or Amy. Why's she coming to this shindig, anyway?"

"The Save the Lighthouse Committee required businesses to buy an entire table for the fundraiser, so she's filling one of our extra seats."

"Gotcha." Gia honked again and then looked through the windshield at the sky. "I still can't believe how early it gets dark here."

"Well, it's a good thing that the streetlight is reflecting off your glitter lip appliqués—otherwise we wouldn't be able to see."

"Silver is understated," she protested in a defensive tone. "I mean, it's not like I'm wearing red or anything."

"Yeah, because red lips are so shocking," I said. "But thank you for taking your pirate eye patch off to drive."

"Sure. But I'm putting it back on when we get to the Smugglers' Tavern. It goes with the theme."

There was a knock on the passenger window.

I jumped when I saw Amy, not because *she'd* startled me but because the puffy sleeves on her homemade yellow prom dress had. As I got out of the car, she whistled like a sailor on shore leave.

"You look like a modern-day Princess Aurora in that pink cocktail dress."

"Thanks, Amy." I searched for an appropriate compliment and came up with, "And you look like the original Snow White."

She giggled like a tickled tween and climbed into the tiny backseat, revealing what looked like white pilgrim shoes.

Or maybe Hester Prynne. I got back into the Ferrari and slammed the door. "Can you drive a little slower now that we have a guest?"

Amy leaned in from the backseat. "Would you? Anything over thirty miles per hour makes me carsick."

"Fine," Gia grumbled as she pulled away from the curb at a crawl. "But next time, you two princesses are taking a horse and carriage."

I looked at Amy through the rearview mirror. "Did you find out anything about Barbicide?"

"Barbicide?" Gia echoed. "Why would you ask her about that?"

"Actually," Amy began, "I'd like to know that too."

"I might as well tell you both." I looked from Gia to Amy. "But what I'm about to say doesn't leave this car, okay?"

"Pinky swear," Gia said, holding out the little finger on her right hand.

We hooked pinkies, and then I held out my finger to Amy.

Her brows knit in confusion, and she raised three fingers. "Scout's honor."

"All right. Gia, today when you brought me the tea at Lucy's station, you put the cup in front of the Barbicide jar. That's when I noticed that the Barbicide level was below the tops of the combs. But they should have been submerged because I'd just topped off all the jars that morning."

"So?" She hooked a left onto Craggy Hill Road where the Smugglers' Tavern was located.

"So, I think Bertha Braun gave Margaret a fatal dose of Barbicide, not blue hair dye."

Gia swerved onto the shoulder, and Amy screamed, wrapping her arms around me from behind.

I peeled Amy off of me and glared at Gia as she eased the Ferrari back onto the road. "You have to learn to control your emotions behind the wheel."

"Who's emotional?" She reached down to the floor of the car. "My Chicken Fillet fell out."

"You've got Chick-fil-A?" Amy asked, her face brightening. "Can I have a bite? I'm starving."

I rolled my eyes. "Chicken Fillets are breast enhancers."

She looked down at her A-cups. "If I'd known that, I would've started eating Chick-fil-A years go."

"You're so literal," Gia exclaimed. "'Chicken Fillets' is the brand name of silicone bra inserts." She retrieved a floppy, flesh-colored disk from the floorboard and handed it to Amy. "Here, this is a Chicken Fillet."

"It looks delicious," Amy said.

I cradled my forehead in my hand. "You know, Gia, maybe those things would stay in better if you wore your bra on the *inside* of your shirt."

"This is too nice a bra to hide under my clothes," she said, pointing to the silver sequined lace. "Besides, it doesn't matter where you wear your bra, as long as you have one on."

I gritted my teeth. "Forget the bra. Can we get back to the Barbicide?"

"Sure," Amy said. "I found a government study on a hairstylist who drank some and turned as blue as—"

"Let's get something straight," I interrupted. "The next person who makes a blue analogy about Margaret Appleby is going to turn as blue as she did, courtesy of my fists."

Amy frowned. "I hope you're not serious, because you just made a blue analogy."

I turned and gave her a half-lidded stare.

She cleared her throat. "Anyway, it turns out that Barbicide is an extremely powerful disinfectant. It's not just a fungicide and a viricide, like it says on the bottle. It's also a germicide and a pseudomonacide."

"What does that mean in regular English?" Gia asked.

Amy blinked. "The same thing it means in scientific English."

I sighed. "And what is that?"

"It kills virtually everything, even the AIDS virus, which is why it's also used in hospitals. And it's durable too. It's the only product of its kind that holds its color after use."

"Margaret would've attested to that," Gia said with a nod in my direction.

I held up my fist, and she turned her eyes back to the road. "Go on, Amy."

She looked at my hand and swallowed. "After ingesting as little as fifty milliliters of Barbicide, acute severe methemoglobinemia occurs within thirty minutes. It's a blood disorder that prevents red blood cells from releasing oxygen to tissues."

"But does this acute severe whatever cause the skin and fingernails to turn blue?" I asked.

"That, and it makes blood turn chocolate brown."

Gia gasped. "Like a blue M&M!"

I leaned across the console and punched her in the arm.

"Careful, *cug*! I'm trying to drive up a hill, here."

"'Trying' is definitely the word for it," I said, rubbing my knuckles. "What else, Amy?"

She crossed her arms to protect her biceps. "If not treated quickly, the nervous system goes into shock, and then the person lapses into a coma and dies."

"How do you treat it?" I asked.

"With Methylene blue."

"More blue?" Gia exclaimed as she parked behind a line of cars along the side of the road. "Is that really a good idea?"

I silenced her with a look, although I had the same question. "Did you happen to find out how much Barbicide it takes to kill someone?"

Amy pushed up her glasses. "According to the study, fifty milliliters, which is a little over an ounce and a half."

"That's about the amount that was missing from Lucy's jar," I noted. "Maybe a little less."

"So now what?" Gia asked, snapping her eye patch into place.

"I'm not sure," I said. "But when we go into the tavern, keep your eyes—well, your eye, Gia—and ears open. Practically everyone in town is going to be there, and you can bet they'll be talking about what happened to Margaret Appleby."

Gia pulled her makeup case from her orange Moschino bag, dusted herself with bronzer, and then doused herself in Prada Candy perfume.

Amy started coughing and clutched at her throat.

"Seriously, Gia," I began, "can you conduct your chemical warfare outside the car?"

"Of course not." She tamped down her lip stickers. "I can't reveal my weapons to the enemy."

Tears streamed down Amy's cheeks as she pinched her nostrils shut. "I can keep my ears open, Cass, but I'm not sure about my eyes. Or my nose."

I grimaced and climbed out of the car. There was no way I was going to catch a killer with these two as my sidekicks.

Amy scrambled from the backseat, puffed her sleeves, and then hoofed it up the hill like a mountain goat. Gia and I, thanks to our high heels, legged it like camels that had taken a wrong turn out of the desert.

"Why do they call this place the Smugglers' Tavern, anyway?" Gia asked.

"I know," Amy said, trotting back down the hill to join us. "They named it after the smugglers who brought banned English goods and supplies here in the 1800s. The caves they used to store their loot are right below this cliff."

I sniffed. "What a town. Founded by prostitutes, pirates, and smugglers."

Gia nodded. "Just like Atlantic City."

I flashed a wry smile. "What did they smuggle, anyway?"

"Tea, clothes, medicine." Amy raised her finger in the air. "Oh, and during Prohibition, they smuggled moonshine."

"I could use a shot of that now to get me up this road," Gia said.

"But we're practically there," Amy said, pointing to a rustic red brick building up ahead. "Amazing view, isn't it?"

Beyond the tavern lay Danger Cove. The lighthouse was lit, illuminating the dark clouds forming around the gray moon and the black water swirling below.

I shuddered and pulled my pink pashmina scarf around my shoulders. The view seemed more ominous than amazing. "Let's go inside."

Gia pranced up the walkway and opened the door. "We have a reserved table, right?"

"In the name of The Clip and Sip," I replied as I scanned the wood-paneled room. "The confirmation I got from the Save the Lighthouse Committee said it would be in the seating area to the right of the bar toward the back."

"What?" Gia exclaimed. "Why not just put us in the garden outside?"

"I'm sure they weren't trying to hide us," I replied as we headed for the rear of the tavern. Although I had my doubts about that.

To the left of the bar, I spotted an elderly woman sitting at the table reserved for the lighthouse committee. I grabbed Amy by the arm. "Isn't that the mystery writer, Elizabeth Ashby?"

"In the flesh."

"I heard that she was kind of reclusive. What do you suppose she's doing with the committee members?"

"She donated part of the proceeds of her last book, *Murder at the Lighthouse*, to the committee. I'm sure they twisted her arm to get her to sit with them. Speaking of which…" She looked down.

"Oh. Sorry." I released my grip on her bicep and continued toward the back of the tavern. "I don't see an empty table anywhere."

"I think there's a booth behind that big anchor they have on display," Amy said, pointing to a secluded corner. "Maybe that's it?"

My heart sank. Gia was right. They had deliberately placed us out of sight at a table that was probably popular with couples seeking privacy but not with business owners wanting visibility.

Amy rushed ahead and slid into the booth. She gave the vinyl seat a pat. "It sure is cozy."

"Yeah, that anchor really gives us privacy." I took a seat and reached for the drink menu. I needed a stiff shot of something and quick. "Wait. Where did Gia go?"

"She stayed at the bar to hand out some flyers."

My stomach dropped, and I'm pretty sure my blood pressure did too. I didn't know what she was up to, but I knew it wasn't good. I began to study the drink menu in earnest.

"Ahoy there, mateys!" Gia yelled as she flopped down into the seat beside me.

Amy blushed and averted her gaze. "Your silicone is showing."

"Blimey!" Gia shoved a rogue Chicken Fillet back into her bra.

I clenched my jaw. "Drop the pirate parlay and show me one of your flyers."

Her visible eye opened wide, and she went as stiff as a plank. "Uh, I ran out."

"Isn't that convenient?" I leaned forward and pointed a finger at her bra-embellished chest. "If this has anything to do with that Egyptian thing, I swear that I will personally embalm and mummify you for the event."

"Gah, Cass." She frowned as she adjusted a bra strap. "You're so grouchy lately."

I smirked. "Gee, I wonder why."

Her face softened. "Look, I know that the salon is in a crisis, so I decided to take this opportunity to try to drum up some business. The ad you ran in the *Cove Chronicles* came out the same day as that nasty article, so I figured that we could use a plan B."

Now I felt like a wench. "Do you really think anyone will want to come to the salon after two murders?"

"Cassidi's got a point," Amy said, folding her arms on the table.

I scowled. "You stay out of this."

"But I was agreeing with you," she said. "Gia's right. You are *griesgrämig* lately."

"See?" Gia gestured toward Amy. "Try a little optimism. There are people who will go anywhere to get a deal. Take Bree Milford, for example."

"Who?" Amy asked.

"She's the owner of Ocean View Bed & Breakfast, and she's a salon regular," I replied.

"Because she's got an unnatural need to have her eyebrows done once a week," Gia added. "If she can get those two lawns weeded at a discount with a free drink thrown in, she'll step over a dead body to get into the salon."

Maybe she was right. There had to be other people like Bree who would take a chance on The Clip and Sip. We just had to try harder to find them.

"Sorry for the wait, ladies," a thirtyish brunette said. "My name's Hope, and I'll be your server tonight. Can I start you off with something to drink?"

What I really wanted was a Shiner Bock beer from home—with some barbecued brisket and blackberry cobbler smothered in Texas's own Bluebell vanilla ice cream. Wait. Nothing with "blue" in the name.

"You got any grog, lassie?" Gia asked, affecting a pirate accent.

"Uh, no," Hope replied as she passed out menus and bar napkins. "But our drink special tonight is a Creole Custa, which is a rum and fruit base infused with chili."

Gia stuck her tongue out. "Fruit and chili? Where are we, Mexico? We'll just take a round of good old-fashioned coconut vodka shots, please."

"And three Rainier beer chasers," I added.

"Coming right up," Hope said. She grinned at Gia before heading for the bar.

"Did you see that?" Gia flailed her arm in Hope's direction. "She gave me a funny look, just like everyone else here. They're all staring at us, you know."

"How?" I asked, gesturing toward the anchor.

"They can see us when they walk by."

I put my finger to my lips. "Maybe they can't peel their eyes off your pirate patch and disco-ball mouth."

"Or they're bedazzled by your bra," Amy added.

"Then it's because they recognize fashion when they see it," Gia said, taking a sideways glance at Amy's Snow White sleeves.

Oblivious to Gia's jab, Amy reached for the menu. "What's everyone getting to eat? They make a mean basket of fish and chips."

Gia wrinkled her lips. "Nothing. I've got *agita*."

Amy furrowed her brow. "They're going to have a band tonight. Maybe you should work off your nervous energy on the dance floor."

"Not *agitated*," I said. "*Agita*. It's New Jersey Italian for heartburn."

Gia frowned. "I think I ate some spoiled *gabigol*."

"You ate garbage?" Amy closed her menu. "Well, that explains why you have heartburn."

"What she means is that she ate some *capicola*, an Italian deli meat."

Amy scratched her head. "I'm not sure I can keep my ears open either, Cass."

"Oh, dear Lord," I mumbled.

Gia stood up and lifted her eye patch. "Who's that hottie with Zac Taylor?"

"Where?" Amy shot from her seat like a cannon.

I slid from the booth and hid behind the anchor, peering around one side. Zac and a friend were seated at the bar and surrounded by bottled blondes—in dire need of root jobs, I might add. "Well, he certainly doesn't look injured."

"What?" Gia asked.

"Nothing," I snapped. I was in no mood to tell her about Clyde Willard and the boat-repair accident at the Pirate's Hook Marine Services, especially since Zac was clearly in fine form and doing what he did best—hitting on women. "I'm going to the ladies' room. I'll be right back."

Of course, I didn't need the bathroom. What I needed was a break. I headed toward the restrooms but then slipped out a door marked *Beer Garden* for a breath of fresh air.

As I stepped outside into the night, a ship's horn blared in the distance. Perhaps because of the gloom, the deck was empty. I took a seat at the first table to my right, which was directly behind a massive pine tree that had been preserved in the middle of the deck. Then I leaned my head against the red brick wall of the building, closed my eyes, and took a deep breath.

"It was that Conti girl," a male voice whispered from the darkness. "She's been asking questions."

I bolted upright. The voice came from straight ahead, but I couldn't see who it was because of the tree.

"You don't say," a female said.

I froze. I knew that voice. It belonged to Bertha Braun. But who was the man?

"For the record, you've been duly warned," he said in a low voice.

"Just why *are* you warning me?"

He sighed. "It's the right thing to do."

"And we know that you always do the right thing," she sneered.

The ship horn blasted again, and the pair fell silent.

I seized the moment to tiptoe to the tree. I held my breath and peeked around the wide trunk. The man was Dr. Windom!

A crowd of people came onto the deck, and I slunk behind them to the back door. As soon as I stepped inside, I came face to face with PTA mom and meddler extraordinaire, Mallory Winchester.

She crossed her arms. "I saw you spying on that couple just now. I can't say I'm surprised to learn that you're a voyeur."

"Likewise," I said as I pushed past her—okay, shoved—and hurried to the table.

"Guess who showed up?" Amy asked, elbowing an already uncomfortable-looking Lucy.

"I'm so glad you came," I said. "But—"

"I tried to order her a drink so that we could all make a toast," Gia interrupted, "but she doesn't want one."

Lucy smoothed the skirt of her green goddess-style dress and attempted a smile. "I'm just here to support the salon."

"I appreciate that," I said. "But something's come up, and we need to leave."

"We just got here," Amy whined.

"It's important. Trust me."

Gia looked me in the eye and nodded. "Let's toast to the salon and then split."

"If we're going to toast to anything," I began, "it should be to Margaret's memory."

Gia raised her glass. "*Salud*!"

I looked at her open-mouthed. "*Health*? That's how you toast her?"

Duncan Pickles appeared from behind the anchor wearing a *Cove Chronicles* press pass and holding a highball glass. "To properly toast Margaret Appleby, you should have ordered a round of blue sharks."

Amy's eyes narrowed. "Why would we order those?"

"Because, as it turns out, Margaret Appleby was worth a small fortune," he replied. "Three million dollars, to be precise."

This was news to me. From all appearances, Margaret had lived a modest life. She wore inexpensive clothes, took public transportation to the salon, and always asked me for the senior-citizen discount. "What does that have to do with us?"

Duncan slipped his free hand into the pocket of his slacks. "Based on my investigation, I'd say you turned the old lady blue because you're all a bunch of money-hungry sharks. Your business is failing, your cousin here wants to start her own business, and Lucy's been trying to get enough money together to move to Sweden and marry a chef."

"Like *the* Swedish Chef?" Gia's eyes danced. "Why did no one tell me this?"

I put my hand over her mouth and glowered at Duncan. "You can't possibly think that we did something to Margaret."

"I don't know whether you were all in on it or not." He looked at Lucy. "But I know *you* were. Why'd you do it? Were you trying to get money out of Margaret, and she refused? Maybe she even threatened to report you to the police?"

Amy stood up and clenched her fists. "Does Lucy look like the type of person who could extort money from a little old woman and then murder her?"

"No, but she was convicted of felony assault," he said.

Felony assault? I looked at Lucy, who'd turned as green as her dress.

"I... It's true." She lowered her head. "I pulled a girl's hair for trying to kiss Sven at our senior prom, and her mother pressed charges."

"That's it?" Gia exclaimed. "You yanked some chick's hair?" She rolled her eyes. "Well, then I should be in the slammer for socking Tina Squarcialupi at my prom after she threw pizza on my dress."

Amy's chin started to wobble. "At least you girls got to go to the prom."

"All right. Time to go," I announced. I had to get Lucy—and Gia and Amy—out of the tavern before this situation deteriorated any further. "Please step aside, Mr. Pickles. We'd like to leave."

"So soon?" He gazed at me over the rim of his glass as he took a sip of his drink. "I thought we could sit and chat for a moment."

Amy grabbed Gia's purse, pulled out the Prada, and drenched Duncan.

"What the—" He stepped backward and rubbed his eyes.

"Serves you right, *sauertopf*!" Amy shouted. "Let's roll, ladies."

As we hurried from the tavern, my mind was reeling, and it wasn't from Gia's perfume—at least not entirely. I couldn't fathom the ramifications of Lucy's arrest record on her current situation, but now I understood why the police were focusing on her. The question was—what did Lucy's prior conviction mean for Bertha? If Bertha had poisoned Margaret, would she get away with murder? And if she did, what did that mean for me? Now that Dr. Windom had tipped her off, she knew that I suspected her of killing Margaret. Given Bertha's history, that could only mean one thing.

I could be next on her hit list.

CHAPTER SEVEN

The view up Gia's skirt as she knelt on the high countertop of our living room bar only served to underscore the double entendre of the original, hand-carved *Bottoms Up* name placard hanging on the wall above.

"Want some cake vodka?" she called as she rummaged in a cabinet.

"Definitely not." I kicked off my heels and curled up on the pink sheet covering our crimson Victorian couch. "I need to keep a clear head."

She hopped to the floor with a highball glass in one hand and raised a jar of Betty Crocker white icing with the other. "I've got frosting to go with it."

"You're actually going to eat frosting with that?"

"Yeah," she replied with a shrug. "And if I had frosting vodka, I'd eat cake with it."

I cocked a brow. "Why not simplify and have iced cake vodka instead?"

Gia pulled a bottle from the mirrored bar. "Because that's not good for you," she explained as she poured a few inches of vodka into her glass. "You need to have something in your stomach when you drink."

I chewed my thumbnail and then mumbled, "Right now I couldn't put a thing in my stomach."

"Well, I can. It's seven o'clock, and I haven't had dinner." She took a seat beside me and placed the frosting between her thighs.

"What about your *agita*?"

"Everyone knows that sugar kills acid. That's why you put a teaspoon in tomato sauce." She placed her glass on the end table and turned on the fringed fuchsia lamp. "So, did Bertha kill your appetite?"

I nodded. "Even if she's not the murderer, you know she's vindictive. Now that she knows I suspect her, she'll get even."

Gia popped the top off her frosting. "I still can't believe that douchebag doctor would tell her about your visit. Talk about breaking patient privacy laws."

I gave her a look. "Do you really think Dr. Windom would worry about my privacy when a murder is involved?"

"Are you saying that you think they're in on this together?"

"I'm not sure." I pulled a gold pillow to my chest. "But it sounded like he was just letting her know out of a sense of obligation."

Gia spooned a glob of frosting into her mouth, took a sip of vodka, and swished it around. "Well." She stopped to swallow. "I think we learned one thing for sure tonight."

"What's that?"

She pointed her spoon at me. "You need to start doing background checks on your employees."

"Okay, I deserve that. But you're not suggesting that Lucy killed Margaret, are you?"

"I don't know." She jabbed the spoon into the thick frosting. "I still think she acted weird during the 9-1-1 call. And now that I know she's a convicted hair puller, I'm even more suspicious."

"Let me get this straight," I said, turning to face her. "You're more suspicious of Lucy for pulling someone's hair than you are of Bertha for poisoning a patient?"

Gia licked some frosting from her tiger-striped fingernail. "Well, yeah. I mean, Lucy was in cosmetology school her senior year."

"So?"

She rolled her eyes at my cluelessness. "So, what kind of stylist pulls hair, especially in the age of extensions? That's just wrong."

It goes without saying that I saw the fault in Gia's logic. But as a stylist myself, I had to agree with her about one thing—extensions were off-limits.

"And," she continued, "the fact that Bertha gave some woman medicine that she was allergic to doesn't make her a killer."

"I get that." I rested my chin on the pillow as Dee's words of warning came to mind. "But it certainly shows that Bertha's capable of going to extremes when she's mad. And we have no idea how far she'll go."

"If you're so worried, then why don't you go to the police?"

"And tell them what?" I exclaimed, tossing the pillow at the arm of the couch. "I don't have any proof against Bertha, and they already know about the incident with the patient since Dr. Windom reported it."

She tapped the spoon against her bottom lip. "You could tell them about the Barbicide."

"Then they'd probably accuse Lucy of using it since it was right there on her station." I stood up and started pacing in front of the fireplace. "Besides, if I'm right about the Barbicide, then the lab will find it in Margaret's system soon enough. You heard Amy say how indestructible the stuff is, and there can't be too many substances that make you turn as blue as... Well, never mind."

I flopped back onto the couch, causing Gia to spill her vodka.

"Crap!" She jumped up and began removing the wet sheet from the couch.

"Sorry. But you can leave it. The alcohol will actually kill the cooties instead of just covering them."

"What you need are furniture condoms," Gia said, heading for the bar with her empty glass.

"Did you have to use that term?" I huffed. "All I want is for this to be a nice, normal home and salon."

"It's never going to be normal, Cass." She poured herself another inch of vodka. "Not even if you gut the place."

That was the understatement of the century. Or, in this case, of the past century and a half.

Gia raised her glass and took a sip of vodka, sans frosting. "But it is nice. Whenever you watch one of those home renovation shows, they rave about Victorians that have the original fixtures and furniture like yours does. I'll bet that home renovator from Finials and Facades would tell you the same thing. By the way, didn't she say that these houses were called 'painted ladies'?"

"Yes, but I'd rather avoid that phrase for obvious reasons. And I guess I hadn't thought about the place that way," I admitted, although I was confident that as a renovator and a woman, Alex Jordan would understand my cootie concerns about the furniture.

"Maybe it's time you did." She took a seat in a violet, velvet high-back chair. "It would be so much easier to just embrace its history, like Vinnie did."

I glanced around the room. Now that the Sadie statue had been removed, it wasn't half-bad—except for the picture of Hope, Faith, and Charity above the fireplace, of course. There was the little matter of the floor-to-ceiling—and just ceiling—gilt mirrors, not to mention a tall coffee table against the wall that might not have ever been a coffee table, if you get my drift. But the furniture did have a lot of character (some of which I hoped that a good steam cleaning would remove). And there was an antique player piano next to the bar.

"The only thing I would get rid of," Gia began, "is that picture of Hope and the girls. I always feel like they're looking right at me."

"That's what bothers you about it? Not the brazen beaver shots?"

"It's not my policy to stare at people's privates," she said with a pointed look. "And anyway, why haven't you given that thing to Amy yet?"

"Because it's bolted down, and I haven't gotten around to figuring out how to remove it."

Gia brought the glass to her lips and then froze. "Why would anyone bolt down a picture?"

"I imagine things got pretty wild in here. I mean, the clients were all loggers."

She leapt from the chair as though she'd been pinched by a lumberjack. "Vinnie's money! I'll bet it's behind the picture." She grabbed a stool from the bar and placed it next to the fireplace. "Quick, get me a big wrench."

"Do I look like I have a wrench?"

"Right." She removed the spoon from her jar of frosting, licked it clean, and then jammed the handle between the frame and the wall.

I moved to the edge of my seat. I didn't want to get my hopes up about a possible cash stash, but it *was* weird that the picture was secured. "What are you going to do? Pry it off the wall?"

Gia pressed her head and shoulder into the wall and tried to peer behind the photo. "First I'm going to work the spoon around the frame and see if I feel something."

"Okay. But if you damage that thing, you'll have to answer to Amy."

"She still has to answer to me for dumping my Prada Candy on Duncan. That stuff ain't cheap, even though it's made to make you smell like you are." She climbed from the stool and moved it to the opposite side of the frame. "But if I find the money, I'll be able to buy myself all the Prada I want, perfume and otherwise."

At the mention of unlimited Prada, my heart fluttered in my chest. "Just how much money are we talking?"

"Well, my dad told me that Vinnie bragged to him about some side business he had that was super lucrative. But Carla once said that she wouldn't be surprised if he had ties to the Atlantic City Mafia. If the mob angle is true, then we could be talking millions."

I fell backward against the couch. My aunt Carla had never mentioned that bombshell to me, but I didn't talk to her very often—or my father, for that matter—since they both lived in New Jersey. But now I was starting to wonder whether Uncle Vinnie had been whacked.

Gia inserted the spoon into the bottom of the frame. "It's really tight here." She paused as she tried to move the spoon forward. "Now it's stuck."

"Maybe the bolt is tighter on that end." I stood up and held the stool for support.

She grasped the spoon with both hands and pulled downward. When it finally came out, a black daily planner slipped from behind the frame and fell to the floor.

We stared down at the book like it was a nineteenth-century prostitute back from the dead.

"Holy freakin' cannoli," Gia breathed as she climbed from the barstool. "I think it's one of those little black books that men always talk about in old 1950's movies." She picked it up and began to flip through the pages. "But it has a bunch of men's names in it."

I looked over her shoulder. "Maybe it's the brothel's client list?"

She turned to the front of the book. "It was printed in 2013, so it had to be Vinnie's."

My eyes widened. "He slept with men too?"

"Please!" Gia waved. "Based on what I've heard about him and the so-called 'ladies of Danger Cove,' he wouldn't have had the time or the energy."

"Yeah." I put my hands on my hips. "Because it's not like he discriminated based on age."

"Hey. Look at this," she said, pointing to a page. "Beside the list of names there's a column of numbers marked *bd.* Whaddaya suppose the *bd* stands for?"

"Uh, *birthday*?"

"Nah, it's probably two words."

I bent my head in thought. "Oh my gosh." I grabbed Gia's arm. "Do you think it stands for *blue dye*?"

Gia went completely still, and then she shook her head. "It can't be. I mean, what would all these numbers represent? The bottles of blue hair dye these men were buying from The Yankee Clipper? You and I both know that there just aren't that many people wanting blue hair."

"Yeah, and there wouldn't be any reason to hide the book, either. So, do you think those numbers have to do with money? Like for bets or something?"

"That's it!" Gia snapped the book shut. "Vinnie was a bookie! And this is a record of the bets he was placing for his clients in Atlantic City."

"Maybe the *b* is for 'bets,' and the *d* could be for dollars. So, like 'bet dollars' or 'bet in dollars'?"

"You're a natural-born sleuth, Cass."

"But this is all just conjecture."

Gia sat on the barstool. "No, we're onto something. I can feel it. And you have to admit that it fits with what Carla said about the mob."

I hated to think that my uncle could have been involved in organized crime, but it wasn't out of the realm of possibility. The Mafia had a long and storied history in Atlantic City. "If he was mixed up with the mob, do you think they put a hit on him for some reason?"

She nodded. "And maybe Margaret too."

"Here at the salon?" I sank onto the couch. "I can't believe that."

Gia shook the book at me. "If the two of them were connected, then it's possible. And you heard what Duncan said about Margaret's millions. How did a little old lady get so much money?"

"Those are good questions," I said as I massaged my temples to keep my head from spinning. "But I still need some kind of proof."

She threw her arms into the air. "Then let's go get it."

I looked up, surprised. "Where?"

"Margaret's house," she said, flipping her hair. "Where else?"

"Gia, we can't just go break in. That's a crime."

She crossed her arms. "Would you do it if your life depended on it?"

"Well, of course, but—"

"Then go change," she said, pointing in the direction of my room. "Bring a pair of gloves, and wear something dark and slinky."

I stared at her as the horrible reality dawned on me—Gia, my happy-go-lucky cousin who saw only life's possibilities and never its problems, thought my life was in danger.

I stood up on shaky legs and did as I was told.

* * *

"This place looks even more like a friggin' gingerbread house than Amy's," Gia whispered as we crouched behind an ocean spray bush in back of Margaret's thatched Victorian cottage. "I wouldn't be surprised if the windowpanes were made of sugar."

"We can always go back to the car," I said, hoping she'd agree. I hadn't stopped shaking since we'd arrived, and it had nothing to do with the chilly night air.

"We came here for evidence, and we're not leaving until we get some. Now, wait here while I try to find a way inside."

"Gladly," I muttered. While Gia worked her way around the house, I tried to formulate a search strategy. The problem was that I had no idea what we were looking for. It was possible that Bertha had sent Margaret a threatening letter or something along those lines. But I didn't have the faintest idea what would tie her to my uncle. A betting ticket? Or a hotel receipt? I shivered—this time from disgust.

"Cass," Gia whisper-shouted.

I poked my face out of the bush. "What?"

She made an obscene Italian gesture that involved the crook of her elbow. "Come here, will ya?"

I came out from behind the bush and followed her around the side of the house.

Gia interlaced her gloved fingers and bent over. "Gimme your foot so I can hoist you up to the window."

"Why am I going in first?" I whisper-protested. "This was your idea."

"Because it's your salon and your skin we're trying to save."

I remembered Bertha's threat to make a skin quilt out of Margaret and stepped into Gia's hands.

After considerable grumbling, grunting, and groaning, she lifted me just enough so that I could open the window. Then I gripped the ledge and used my rusty monkey-bar muscles to pull my torso inside.

As I paused to let my eyes adjust to the darkness, Gia grabbed my legs and gave my backside a shove. I shot forward over a sink and landed hands and face first on a linoleum floor. I lay on my belly, fantasizing about pushing her off a cliff. "You do that again," I warned in a low voice, "and it's your skin you'll be needing to save."

"I thought you were stuck," she whisper-called from outside.

And I swear I heard her suppress a giggle.

I checked my wrists for fractures, lumbered to my feet, and pulled my phone from my back pocket. I tapped the flashlight icon and discovered that I was in the kitchen. After closing the window, I located the back door and then hesitated before unlocking it. What I really wanted was to leave Gia out back, but I decided that I needed her help even if she was a *stunad* (New Jersey Italian for "moron").

I opened the door, and she pranced in like everything was okay between us. I shined my light in her eyes, interrogation style. Because she'd been waiting for me in the car when we left the house, it was the first time I'd gotten a good look at her. And I wasn't prepared for what I saw. "*What* are you *wearing*?"

She looked down at her Catwoman suit. "It's my spying outfit."

There were a lot of questions I could ask, but I started with, "What's up with the cat ears and tail?"

"If someone sees me, they'll think I'm a cat."

I snorted. "A really, really big one."

She narrowed her eyes. "Are you calling me fat? Because I could totally be a panther."

I shined my light on the lower half of her body. "With opera gloves, a shiny gold belt, and black stiletto boots?"

"If I get caught, I want to look put together, all right?" Gia turned on her phone light and flashed it around the room. "Whoa! Look at that."

I started. "What is it?"

"Margaret had a blueberry theme in her kitchen. Go figure."

"Never mind that, Julie Newmar," I quipped, although I did think the blueberry thing was more than a little ironic. "I'll search the living room, and you search the bedroom, okay?"

"Purrfect," she replied as she pussyfooted through the adjoining living room and up the flight of stairs in the entryway.

Meanwhile, I surveyed the living room. It looked a lot like my German grandma's sitting room in Fredericksburg, except that there was no cuckoo clock. In its place, a grandfather clock towered over an extra-wide beige armchair and a matching ottoman. On one side of the chair was a basket full of knitting needles and yarn, and on the other a stack of newspapers and magazines. The item that caught my eye, however, was a built-in bookshelf that covered an entire wall. Books were the perfect hiding place for letters and other documents.

I don't know what I was expecting Margaret to read, maybe cozy mysteries or the usual classics like *Little Women* and *Gone with the Wind*. But as I scanned the titles on her shelf, I was more convinced than ever that she wasn't at all who she had seemed. *The Anarchist Cookbook*, *Lolita*, *American Psycho*, *The Satanic Verses*, *Slaughterhouse-Five*—it read like a catalogue of the world's most controversial novels.

"Just goes to show you that you really can't judge a book by its cover," I muttered as I began flipping through the pages of *Harry Potter and the Sorcerer's Stone*.

I must have gone through at least a hundred books when the grandfather clock struck nine and I practically jumped from my skin. I hadn't found anything—not a letter, a picture, or even a note scribbled in a margin. I was starting to think that this whole escapade had been futile, but I resolved to finish going through the books before I gave up.

I reached for *Mother Goose Tales* just as Puss in Boots sashayed down the stairs.

"That bedroom is like a hospital room," Gia began, stopping to lean over the railing, "and the bathroom is practically a pharmacy. You should see the pills in there, Cass. And I'm not kidding when I say that she could stock the laxatives aisle at Walgreens."

I put my hand on my hip. "Did you look in all the boxes and prescription bottles?"

"Every one."

"What about the top of the closet and under the bed?"

"I searched the whole upstairs, even her underwear drawer, and I'm not sure I'll ever live it down." She shook her head. "It gives a whole new meaning to the phrase 'granny panties.'"

At least there was no lingerie. "Why don't you go start on the kitchen?"

"Sure." She stepped into the entryway and stopped dead in her tracks.

The back door was making a creaking sound.

Gia and I froze and exchanged a look. Someone was in the kitchen.

We ran to the dining room on the other side of the stairs. Gia hid beside a china cabinet, and I knelt behind the wide wooden base of the round table.

I looked back to make sure that Gia was out of sight. I couldn't see her, but her tail was sticking out. *That darn cat!*

The footsteps became louder as the intruder walked from the kitchen to the living room. Then the person stopped in the area of the bookshelf. Next I heard the unmistakable sound of flipping pages and books hitting the hardwood floor.

Maybe I'd been on the right track after all.

I didn't need to look to know that Bertha was the intruder, but I did need to see anything that she might find.

I tucked my hair behind my ear and, at the speed of a snail, leaned to one side to peer around the pedestal base of the table.

And I almost fell over.

The intruder was Clyde Willard from Dr. Windom's office!

CHAPTER EIGHT

Stifling a scream, I ducked back behind the pedestal. Fear surged through my body like liquid ice. Clyde had narrow, shifty eyes, and his face had a weathered look to it—the kind that attested to a hard life and an even harder disposition. I was scared of Bertha, but I was terrified of Clyde, even though he did have one arm in a sling.

Even in the darkness, Clyde looked rough. He had an angry scowl on his face, and with every book he pulled from the shelf, his anger seemed to grow. He growled and grunted like a wild animal as he tore through pages and hurled books across the room.

The madder Clyde got, the more afraid I became. My breath was coming in bursts, a sign that a panic attack was looming, and the thudding sounds of the flying books weren't helping me any.

Leaning my forehead on the cold, wooden pedestal, I tried to calm myself. I couldn't fall apart, because Gia was depending on me. And despite the Catwoman getup she was wearing, she definitely didn't have nine lives.

The glare of a flashlight lit up the living room, and the house fell eerily silent.

Had Clyde found what he'd come for?

Logic dictated that I stay as still as a statue, but curiosity killed the cat—or the cat's sidekick, as it were. I had to know what he was looking at, and as I peeked around the pedestal, I hoped like heck that it wasn't me.

Clyde's head was bent over a book. The light from his flashlight illuminated his forearm, exposing purplish-brown spots, probably from the accident at the Pirate's Hook Marine Services.

I was trying to make out details of the cover when he threw the book in the direction of the kitchen.

"Where is it, Leona?" he yelled.

Leona? For a moment, I wondered whether he was in the wrong house. But that couldn't be right, because he'd asked for Bertha by name at Dr. Windom's office, so I was all but certain that they were in this together. Leona was probably a third accomplice. But what was the "it" they were after? And why did Clyde think that he would find it on Margaret's bookshelf? It wasn't like she could have hidden her millions in a book. Maybe it was a key to a safe-deposit box?

The boom of the bookshelf slamming to the ground shook me from my thoughts.

Gia gasped, but Clyde didn't appear to notice. After overturning the shelf, he proceeded to destroy Margaret's living room. He overturned furniture, shattered lamps and knickknacks, and even pulled the pictures off the walls. When he was done, he glanced around the room as though surprised by his own actions. Then he ran his hand through his thinning hair and stepped into the entryway.

Cowering behind the pedestal, I held my breath and willed Gia to keep quiet. And I waited.

Seconds passed, but they seemed like hours. Finally, I heard the sound of Clyde's footsteps. He was climbing the stairs.

I let out a long, slow exhale. Then I sprung into action. I reached behind me and pulled Gia's tail.

A cat ear appeared from behind the cabinet, followed by an eye.

I put my finger to my lips and motioned for her to follow me.

For once in her life, she kept her mouth shut and did as I suggested. Maybe the cat got her tongue.

We tiptoed through the entryway and into the dismantled living room. As I made my way around the ottoman, which was now lying on its side, I caught the hem of my pants on a nail. Frantic, I reached down to free myself and saw that the bottom of the ottoman was covered with a thin sheet of craft plywood, rather than the usual fabric. And it was detaching from the base.

A crash came from upstairs as Clyde began wreaking his room-wrecking havoc, and I jumped so high that I freed my pant leg.

Come on, Gia mouthed from the kitchen doorway.

I motioned for her to go ahead. Then, emboldened by the noise from upstairs, I peeled back the plywood, and a Bible tumbled out.

Could this be what Clyde was looking for? It didn't seem likely. Then again, my grandmother wrote important family information in her Bible. Maybe Margaret had done the same. But why would she feel the need to hide something like that? More importantly, why would Clyde want to find it?

The sounds from upstairs stopped, and the house went silent.

I scooped up the Bible and heard Clyde's footsteps cross the second floor toward the stairs. As I rushed toward the kitchen, I saw that Gia had exited through the window, probably to avoid making the door squeak. Channeling her Catwoman costume, I took a catlike leap, landed on all fours on the countertop, and sprung outside. When I dropped to the ground below, Gia pounced and pulled me up by the wrist.

And we ran like cats out of hell.

* * *

When Amy came to unlock the library door at eight o'clock sharp and saw me standing on the other side, her quasi unibrow almost split apart in surprise.

Okay, so I wasn't exactly a frequent visitor, especially not first thing on a Saturday morning.

She turned the key in the lock and threw open the door. "Look what the cat dragged in."

You don't know the half of it, I thought, still ruing my decision to let Gia talk me into going to Margaret's house. "I was hoping to get your help with something. Is now a good time? Or is Ben around?"

"He's here, but he's in the office with Betty Snodgrass from the Danger Cove Rose Society," Amy whispered, depositing a massive set of keys into her skirt pocket. "Now that she's president, she's trying to root out all the books in our catalogue that promote native-only plants as a water-conservation method. She claims that they discriminate against people who plant nonnative species of roses and other flowers."

"Wow," I said as I slipped out of my red pea coat. "That's taking it kind of far."

"I know." Her face blossomed into a smile. "She's a real thorn in Ben's side," she joked, elbowing me in the ribs. "Get it, Cass?"

"Yeah, I got it, all right." I frowned and rubbed *my* side. "Speaking of pains," I began, with emphasis, "I've been up all night trying to decipher some notes I came across."

She pushed the book cart away from the overnight return slot and headed for the information desk. "That reminds me, how did you do on that quiz?"

"I should get the results today," I said, following her to the counter. I plucked a red thread from my short black skirt and added, "But I wasn't talking about accounting notes."

She reached into the bottom of the cart for returned books. "Did you enroll in another class?"

I hesitated. Amy was scrupulously honest, so I wasn't sure how she was going to take the news of my cat caper with Gia. "Actually, I was reading Margaret's Bible."

She tucked some books under her arm and reached back into the cart. "How did you get her Bible?"

"Uh, I found it." That was the truth, after all.

"Where was it?" she asked, rising from the cart with a load of books. "Under the hair dryers?"

I scrunched up my face and tried to look as repentant as I felt. "It was in her house."

Amy dropped the books onto the counter. "You broke into her house and stole her Bible?" She put her hands on her hips. "Well, if you had to steal a book, I'm glad you took that one, because it sounds like you need a refresher on the Ten Commandments."

I put my coat and tote bag next to the pile of books and looked her straight in the eye. "You know that I would never do anything like that under normal circumstances. But Gia and I were looking for evidence tying Margaret to Bertha or my uncle."

"I should have known Gia was behind this." She picked up a scan gun and ran it over a book barcode. "She's always coming up with some wacky scheme or other."

I couldn't argue with her there, but I was obliged to defend my cat-suited cousin. "She was just trying to help me, and I think we found something important. The bad thing is that while we were there, this man broke in, and he might've seen me when I was leaving."

Amy stopped scanning. "Do you know who he was?"

I nodded. "His name is Clyde Willard."

"Oh no!" She dropped the scanner. "You'd better hope he didn't see you."

My mouth went dry. "Why? Do you know him?"

"Yes, and he's a real *tunichtgut*," she replied as though that were self-explanatory.

"I heard *gut* in there," I said in a hopeful tone. "That's *good,* right?"

"Not in this case. It means that he's a ne'er-do-well." She checked in another book. "Clyde came in here looking for odd jobs once, and Ben turned him down because some of the library patrons said that he had a habit of borrowing things he didn't return."

"That doesn't sound *so* bad," I said.

Amy pursed her lips and pointed the scan gun at me. "Not after you break into a house and steal a Bible, it doesn't. But some of our female patrons claim that he's also a peeping Tom, and that's definitely not *gut*."

The thought of Clyde staring into my window made my skin crawl. I shuddered and changed the subject. "By the way, do you have any patrons named Leona? Or do you know anyone in Danger Cove by that name?"

"That doesn't ring a bell, but I'll check." She put the scanner on the counter and began typing into the computer. "There's no Leona in our database, and I couldn't find one on whitepages.com, either."

"That's interesting, because I heard Clyde refer to a Leona last night. Do you think it's Margaret's middle name?"

Amy typed "Appleby" into the library database. "According to her registration information, it's Mae."

"Huh. I guess this Leona could be from out of town." As soon as I'd said it, a thought occurred to me. I pulled Margaret's Bible from my tote bag and opened the cover. "And maybe she has something to do with this."

Amy took the book and began to browse the handwritten notes on the inside flap. "It's a list of babies and their birth dates."

"Thirty of them, to be exact. And since they were all born between 1980 and 1985, and they all have different last names, they can't possibly be Margaret's relatives."

"And they were all named 'Baby,' like Jennifer Grey in *Dirty Dancing*," she said, running her finger down the list. "I guess that was a popular name in the eighties."

I rolled my eyes. "No, it's what they do in hospitals. They call a newborn 'Baby Smith' or 'Baby Jones.' Which makes me wonder if maybe Margaret helped deliver those babies. Do you know what she did for a living before she retired?"

"As far as I know, she hasn't worked since I've been here." She sat on the tall stool behind the computer. "But I doubt that she was a doctor, because she never used the title. And if she was a nurse, you'd think that she would've delivered more than thirty babies."

"Unless she lived in a really small town," I said, thinking of Fredericksburg. "Or if she was a midwife."

"This might not have anything to do with birthing babies. Maybe she was a pastor, and these were babies she baptized."

I leaned my forearms on the counter. "Whatever this list is, I think it has something to do with her death."

Amy furrowed her brow. "Why?"

"Because Margaret had it hidden in an ottoman and because Clyde was searching through all of her books."

She scanned the surnames. "But the name Willard isn't on this list."

"Neither is the name Braun, but that doesn't mean anything."

"So, you think Clyde and Bertha are both involved in Margaret's murder?"

"It sure looks that way to me, but I don't know how I could prove it." I drummed my fingernails on the countertop as I tried to think of my next investigative move. Then I bolted upright. "Wait a second!"

She pushed up her glasses. "For what?"

"Nothing, it's just an expression. I was thinking of Zac Taylor."

Her jaw dropped. "You think *he's* in on this too?"

I sighed. "Just listen, okay?

She made a lip-zipping gesture and put her hands in her lap.

"When I was at Dr. Windom's office, Clyde said he'd hurt his arm at the Pirate's Hook Marine Services. So, Zac must know him."

"And I'm sure he would be more than happy to help you." She grinned and gave a saucy wink.

I leaned my hip against the counter and crossed my arms. "Now that you put it that way," I said, casting her a sideways look, "I'm not sure I want to talk to him."

Amy stood up. "I don't understand what your problem is with Zac. He's smart, he's a hard worker, and he's hotter than a plate of *senfrostbraten*."

I didn't know what that was, but the word *frost* reminded me of the bleached blondes I'd seen surrounding him at Smuggler's Tavern. "He just seems like a player, and I don't want to get involved with a guy like that."

"If you mean that he's a womanizer, I've never seen any evidence of that."

I gave an incredulous laugh. "Not even you could have missed the crowd of female admirers gathered around him at the bar last night."

Amy sucked in her breath and covered her mouth with her hand. "You're jealous!"

"Don't be ridiculous," I said with what I hoped looked like a nonchalant flip of my hair.

Her grin had practically turned into a leer. "You like him."

"No, I don't," I said, tugging at the neck of my gray sweater. It was getting really hot in here.

"Then prove it by going to talk to him about Clyde."

"I will. I will." I grabbed my tote bag. "But I can't do it right now."

Amy smiled. "Cassidi and Zac sittin' in a tree—"

"Would you stop that?" I interrupted as I picked up the Bible. "The salon reopens in fifteen minutes, so I have to go check on Gia and Lucy before I can go down to the pier."

"K-I-S-S-I-N-G. Fir—" A note died in Amy's throat as I held the Good Book in the air.

"You sing another word," I began, "and you eat this Bible."

She mimed locking her lips and throwing away the key.

I shoved the book into my bag and headed for the door. I felt a twinge of guilt for threatening Amy with the Bible—on a couple of levels. But honestly, sometimes I didn't know which was harder on my sanity—a crazy cousin or a loopy librarian.

I did know one thing, though. I did *not* like Zac Taylor. Not the slightest bit.

* * *

I entered the salon through the back door and deposited my bag on the break room table. It was only nine fifteen, but thanks to last night's break-in and subsequent Bible study, I was already in dire need of a catnap. Uh, scratch that—caffeine. I fired up the espresso machine that we had yet to use on a single client and prepared to make myself a twelve-thousand-dollar cup of coffee.

Gia entered in a New Jersey Devils hockey jersey and high-heel high tops. "Is Lucy with you?"

"Nope." I poured coffee beans into the grinder. "Maybe she's with your pants?"

She smirked. "This jersey is longer than most of the skirts I wear."

"Except that it's not a skirt." I turned on the grinder to underscore my displeasure. I felt bad about being snippy with

Gia, but even though we didn't have any business, I still needed for her to dress as though we did. "Have you tried calling Lucy?"

"Yeah," she replied as she adjusted her red hair-band bow. "But she didn't answer."

"She's probably just running late." I filled the portafilter with the ground coffee and pressed the brew button. "If she doesn't show up in the next twenty minutes, I'll call her. I have to run an errand at the pier, so I need her to relieve me for an hour or so."

Gia took a seat at the table. "I seriously doubt that we'll need either one of you. It's not like we have anything on the schedule." She paused. "But I did book an appointment for next Saturday."

"Really?" I reached into the cabinet for an espresso cup.

She broke into an ear-to-ear grin. "It's a wedding party—six girls, the mother, and the mother-in-law."

"Get out!" I was so psyched that I almost dropped the mini mug. "Why would they call us, though? I mean, not that we're not good enough, but—"

"But we did just kill a client," she said with a curt nod. "Apparently, it was your ad in the paper. The bride's mom said that the wedding is way over budget, and when she figured out how much money they'd save by getting free manicures here, she decided that it was worth the risk to their lives and canceled an appointment she'd made at a swanky salon in Seattle."

I was so excited that I didn't care whether Gia was being sarcastic or sincere. "Given everything Lucy's going through, I'll let her work it solo. Even with the free manicures, I'll still make a good percentage off all those updos."

"Not just that. They want makeup too."

My enthusiasm ebbed. If this bride had been planning to go to a high-end Seattle salon, I was positive that she didn't want to look like Gia's Jersey-inspired idea of a bride. "Did the mother happen to mention her daughter's color scheme?"

She puckered her red-and-black lacquered lips in disgust. "Pink and baby blue. I mean, they really need to throw in some adult colors like red and purple—otherwise this shindig's gonna look like a fancy friggin' baby shower."

As I removed my cup from the espresso machine, I made a mental note to be on hand for the appointment. I wanted to make sure that the bride didn't leave looking like Lily Munster.

Gia snapped her fingers. "I almost forgot. Before the bride's mom called, I took a call from some guy who said he was one of Vinnie's old clients."

I sat across from her at the table. "What did he want?"

"A 'Bobby Darin.' And when I said that I wasn't familiar with that hairstyle, he asked for Vinnie."

"I got the same request a month or so ago," I said, spooning a third of the sugar bowl into my espresso. "It must have been a popular look around here."

"I doubt it. I googled Bobby Darin and found out that he was a 1950's pop singer who went bald when he was like twenty and wore a toupee that looked like a poor man's pompadour. Now, I'm the first one to say that Danger Cove is hopelessly out of style compared to Jersey, but even I have to admit that it's not *that* far behind the times."

I took a quick sip of coffee to hide the smirk on my face.

"The weird thing was," Gia continued, "when I told the guy that Vinnie had passed, he hung up."

"You know, the same thing happened to me. I just assumed that the caller hadn't heard about his death."

She shrugged as the phone began to ring. "I'll get it," she said, heading into the salon. "Maybe it's Lucy."

As I opened my laptop to check my e-mail, I thought back to my conversation with Detective Ohlsen about Uncle Vinnie's former receptionist and those "strange calls" she reported. I wondered whether the callers were saying something unusual to her or whether they were asking for my uncle and then hanging up if he wasn't available. If it was the latter, it could have had something to do with his little black book, especially if Gia was right about him being a bookie. I decided that it was time to bring the book to the police station and let the authorities figure it out.

The second I entered my Gmail account I saw the message that I'd been waiting for—the results of my accounting quiz. I hesitated before opening the e-mail. I'd dropped out of Texas State University when I'd ended up on scholastic probation at the end of my freshman year. Then I'd gone back and dropped out again after the student loans had started piling up. When Uncle Vinnie left me the money, I'd gotten out of debt and back into college. But the online program I'd enrolled in didn't count a lot of my hours from Texas State, so I was still a junior after six years of college. And in my current financial state, I couldn't see spending any more money on school if I wasn't making progress toward the degree. So, my entire college career came down to this moment.

I took a deep breath and clicked the message. The number *50* jumped from the screen. Without batting an eye, I shot the remainder of my espresso as I processed the fact that I'd failed the course. I sat back and said, "I wonder what the future has in store for me now?"

"Funny you should ask," Gia replied from the doorway.

I stared at her in silence. Clearly, I'd spoken too soon.

"That was Lucy's mom," she said, crossing her arms. "She wanted to let us know that Lucy won't be coming in today because the police brought her back to the station an hour ago for more questioning."

I gripped my empty cup, wishing I had another shot of espresso for the bad news that was sure to follow. "Why? Did they find something?"

"The medical examiner did—a puncture wound on Margaret's neck."

My blood ran cold. "Like, from a needle?"

She nodded. "I'll bet that no one noticed it before because it was hidden by her sagging skin." She swallowed and clutched at her throat. "You know what this means, don't you?"

I did, indeed, and it wasn't what Gia was thinking. It meant that the syringe wrapper I'd found in the flower garden might not have belonged to the EMTs after all. It could have come straight from the murderous hands of the killer.

CHAPTER NINE

Ignoring Gia's question, I ran to the garbage can by the back door and flipped the lid. It was empty. I spun around to face my cousin. "What did you do with the trash?"

She looked at me like I'd flipped *my* lid. "I took it out."

I yanked open the door. "One of these days I'm going to take *you* out."

"What did I do?" she exclaimed, jogging behind me as I marched across the parking lot toward the Dumpster. "You're always harping on me to throw out the garbage."

"And the first time you actually did it is the one time I wish you hadn't." I was so upset that I was clenching and unclenching my fists as I walked, but I didn't really blame Gia. I was mad at myself for pitching a potential clue and even madder at the sanitation department for making me share a commercial waste bin with Filippo "Filly" Filipuzzi, the fishmonger next door.

"Look," Gia began after a rare moment of silence, "when I asked you if you knew what the needle mark meant, I was trying to imply that the cops were going to accuse Lucy of injecting Margaret. I didn't mean to suggest that our situation was so desperate that we had to start Dumpster diving."

"That's not what I'm doing," I huffed as we arrived at the bin. "Well, okay, it is. But it's because I threw out a syringe wrapper that might lead us to the killer."

Gia wobbled on her heels. "Whoa. Dude."

"You can say that again," I muttered—not because I'd thrown the wrapper away, but because the stink of rotting fish was assailing my nostrils like a fillet knife.

She took several steps back. "What are you going to do?"

"What do you think?" I kicked off my Candies and started rolling up my pant legs.

She fluttered her red eyelashes. "You're not really going inside that fermented fish pot, are you?"

"Not if you want to do it for me," I replied as I climbed onto the side rail of the bin.

She held up her hands in a stopping motion. "We New Jersey Italians try to avoid 'swimming with the fishes,' especially dead, decomposing ones. Besides, you were the first one who tossed that wrapper."

"That's what I thought you'd say—more or less." I threw my legs over the side of the bin and surveyed the rancid refuse. Our white kitchen bag stood out like a beacon in a foreboding sea of Filly's black, industrial-sized ones.

Holding the side of the bin for support, I eased myself onto the mound of debris. The air was so putrid that I lurched forward and gagged. But I couldn't make any more sudden movements, because if I fell face first into this fowl fish stew, I was going to yack.

Balancing as best I could, I reached for the bag and began picking through its contents—a shampoo bottle, a wad of paper towels, enough hair to make a wig.

"How does it smell in there?" Gia called in a tone evocative of one of the few German words I knew—*schadenfreude*, or pleasure derived from the misfortune of others.

"As sweet as Fredericksburg peach pie," I replied in a honeyed voice.

"You don't have to be sarcastic."

"Don't I?" I pulled an empty bottle from the bag. When I realized that it was the barbeque sauce my mother had sent me from The Salt Lick in Driftwood, Texas, I knew why Gia had taken out the trash.

To get even for this barbeque betrayal, I tossed the bottle against the side of the bin to startle her, and the jerking motion caused the garbage to shift. I lost my balance and stepped backward. My foot sunk deep into a black bag, and fish juice oozed from the opening and puddled around my ankle. I whimpered and looked down in horror.

A dead salmon slid from the bag and stared up at me as if to say, "It's a dog's life, ain't it?"

I dry heaved and swallowed hard.

Gia knocked on the side of the Dumpster. "What's going on in there?"

I gritted my teeth. "What do you think?"

"Well, hurry up, will ya? People in this town have a low-enough opinion of us already. If they see you digging through the Dumpster, we'll never live it down."

She had a point, albeit an incredibly aggravating one. Reluctantly, I resumed my search. I rummaged around in the bag and spotted the wrapper. I started to breathe a sigh of relief, but then I thought better of it. "I found it!"

"Awesome. Now will you come out of there?"

"Gladly." I pulled the wrapper from the bag and discovered that it was stuck to a small pad of paper. Detaching the adhesive portion of the wrapper from the pad, I happened to catch sight of the name and address at the top of the pad. I dry heaved again.

This time, it wasn't the stench of the fish that made me sick—it was the smell of a setup.

"We've got big trouble," I said as I leapt from the bin.

Gia shot me a bored look and ran her fingers through her hair like a Kardashian. "Is this supposed to be news to me or something?"

I held up the pad of paper.

Her face went pale beneath her bronzer. "How did one of Dr. Windom's prescription pads get in our garbage?"

I bit my bottom lip. "It was planted there by the same person who left the syringe wrapper—the killer."

* * *

By late morning, the sun had succumbed to a squadron of black clouds, and yet the atmosphere in the cove was unusually still.

As I walked past the pier toward the Pirate's Hook Marine Services, I couldn't shake the feeling that this was the proverbial calm before the storm—that something awful was looming on the horizon in the wake of the discovery of Dr. Windom's prescription pad. Nor could I shake the smell of that spoiled fish, not even after a long, hot shower, a generous application of orange ginger body mist, and a few sips of Gia's Meyer lemon vodka—for good measure.

When I reached the boat docks in the harbor, a roar from across the bay shattered the quiet.

I scanned the water and spotted a group of sea lions gathered on a flat area of rock near the mouth of the cove. Most of them were resting, but two males were mock sparring and pushing each other with their chests.

"They're awesome, aren't they?" Zac asked.

I stiffened when I realized that he was behind me. I turned and found him standing in front of the service entrance of the Pirate's Hook Marine Services, wiping his hands on a rag. Before I could stop them, my treacherous eyes followed the trail of motor oil down his tight T-shirt and onto his equally tight jeans.

He looked down at his clothes. "Pretty filthy, huh? I'm trying to help one of the guys fix a motor."

My face grew as hot as his smokin' body, and I said the first thing that came to mind. "They *are* awesome." And then, in case he thought that I was talking about his well-developed pecs, I added, "The sea lions, I mean."

He grinned and stuffed the rag into his back pocket. "Believe it or not, the young ones like to body surf."

I laughed. "Really? I would *love* to see that."

"If you come down here often enough you'll see them diving off that rock to catch a wave." He pointed in the direction of the sea lions. "Speaking of the rock, do you see that hook-shaped portion that juts out from where they're laying?"

My eyes lingered on the muscles of his outstretched arm. I shook my head to stop them, and then I nodded in answer to his question.

"It's called Pirate's Hook, because after Bart Coffyn stole that treasure from Sir Francis Drake, they hung him from there in a cage and left him to die."

I wrinkled my lips. "Why would your boss name his business after something so morbid?"

"You mean, my dad," he said. "He started the Pirate's Hook Marine Services as a boat repair shop when he graduated from MIT in 1983. Later on, he branched out into boat sales. And like I told you, he was obsessed with that treasure. In fact, he was convinced that the hook holds the secret to finding it."

My gut told me not to ask, but I didn't always listen to my stomach—unless it wanted food. "Did your father ever go looking for the treasure?"

"Lots of times." He put his hands on his hips and stared out to sea. "But then he died in a car accident when I was in high school, and my mom had to sell the business to the current owner, Clark Graham."

I looked down. "I'm so sorry."

"Don't be," he said with conviction. "It'll belong to my family again one day. I'll see to that."

I fell silent as I thought about how hard it must have been for him and his mother to lose the man they loved and the company that he held so dear. It made my situation with The Clip and Sip seem minor in comparison.

A small smile formed around the corners of Zac's lips, and he looked at me from beneath his long eyelashes. "I didn't see you at the Smugglers' Tavern last night."

The sympathy that I'd felt moments before turned to annoyance. I mean, not only had I been at the tavern, but I'd walked right past him on my way in and out of the joint. Was I really that unnoticeable? "That's funny," I began dryly, "because I saw you."

His eyes opened wide. "How come you didn't say hi?"

I smirked. "Because it looked like you already had plenty of women saying hi to you."

He furrowed his brow, and then his eyes lit up. "Oh, you mean Grace, Helen, and Jackie," he said as though their names would make a difference to me. "They're—"

"Listen," I interrupted in a tone so cold that I practically gave myself frostbite, "I didn't come here to talk about your personal life." Surprised by my own reaction, I adjusted my attitude and added, "I'd like to ask you something that concerns the salon, if possible."

A muscle worked in his jaw, and he shoved his hands into his front pockets. "Sure. Shoot."

I opened my mouth to reply as a door slammed behind me.

"Hey, Zac," a male voice called, "I found that part in the warehouse."

Zac glanced toward the service center. "Be right there, Clyde."

Clyde! A chill shot down my spine. On the off chance that he'd seen me from behind when I was leaving Margaret's house, I needed to leave before he saw my front. "Um, I should let you get back to work. Is there any way I could talk to you tonight? It's important."

"Sorry," he said. "I have plans."

Probably a date with Grace, Helen, or Jackie, I thought. *Or, since they traveled in a pack, maybe with all three.*

"How about breakfast tomorrow?" he continued. "Or, if you'd rather sleep in, we could have brunch."

Sleep. Now there was a tempting thought. But I had to get information about Clyde, and the sooner the better. "Breakfast would be great."

He nodded. "I'll pick you up at eight then."

"Sounds good." I would have preferred to meet him somewhere, but I didn't have time to argue. I had to get going before Clyde got a good look at me. Feigning a shiver of cold, I flashed a wan smile at Zac before pulling my scarf around my face. Then I turned and headed back toward the pier.

Several of the sea lions began barking as I walked away. I knew it was just my imagination, but it surely seemed like they were chasing me off—telling me to leave their friend Zac alone. And now that I thought about it, I had been kind of rude to him about the bleached blondes. It really wasn't any of my business who—or how many—he dated. After all, he was a decent enough guy. He was always willing to help out despite the fact that he'd been through a lot. Plus, anyone who loved animals was a good person, in my book.

"Cassidi!" a female voice called.

Glancing in the direction of the boat docks, I recognized Prudence Miller, the woman who was planning to sail to Alaska. She was waving at me from the bow of a sailboat.

I returned the gesture and made my way down the dock. "Hey, Prudence," I said as I arrived at the sleek vessel. "This is a beautiful boat."

She beamed and gave an affectionate pat to the mast. "This baby's a Catalina C30. I call her *The Sea Hag*." She gave a sheepish smile. "I was a huge fan of the old *Popeye* cartoons when I was little."

I giggled. "I was all about *The Powerpuff Girls*, especially Blossom because she was pink."

"Well, I'm probably a decade older than you, so I'm guessing that was after my time. But enough about me." She made a sweeping motion toward the boat. "Would you like to come aboard and see the cabin?"

I was tempted, but I needed to check on Gia and find out whether there was any news about Lucy. "Can I take a rain check? I have to get back to The Clip and Sip."

"Actually," she began, slipping her hands into the back pockets of her khakis, "I just called you over because I wanted to tell you how sorry I was to hear about what happened to that nice woman, Margaret Appleby."

I bowed my head. "Me too. I can't tell you how bad it feels knowing that she lost her life in my place of business. I also feel bad because the police are going to call you and the other clients in for questioning."

"I've already talked to them. It was no big deal." Prudence stepped onto the dock and put her hand on my back. "I want you to know that there is nothing you could have done to prevent what happened. Besides," she began, her face brightening, "from the way she talked at the salon the other day, she had a full life."

I remembered Margaret mentioning my uncle's tattoo and his "tush," and I cringed on the inside. "I guess."

"Is there any word on the cause of death?"

"Nothing official yet." I hesitated and then added, "But at this point, everyone knows that it was foul play."

She grimaced. "That's one of the worst parts of working in a hospital—tragic cases like this."

The second she mentioned her job, I thought of the syringe wrapper. "Would you mind if I asked you about something I found outside the salon?"

She shook her bangs to one side. "Not at all. What is it?"

"A wrapper from a syringe."

Her head recoiled. "Can I see it?"

I glanced into my purse and then realized that I'd left the wrapper in my bedroom. "I don't have it with me. But what I need to know is whether there's some way to trace the person or the company that bought it."

She drew her index finger to her mouth and thought for a moment. "The manufacturer can trace the batch using the number on the back of the wrapper."

My chest swelled with hope. "Really?"

"Yeah." She crossed her arms. "They would only have general information, though, like the state where the syringe was sold."

"Oh," I said, deflated. "That wouldn't be of much use, I'm afraid. But thanks for your help."

"Absolutely. Please let me know if I can do anything else." She grinned. "I'll be here for a few more days doing some sight-seeing."

"Of course. And if I don't see you before you go, have a safe trip to Alaska." I pulled my purse strap over my shoulder and prepared to leave.

"Cassidi?"

I turned to face her. "Yes?"

"Take care." She gave a wry smile. "Not to be melodramatic, but the world is a dangerous place."

I nodded. "I'm sorry to say this, but Danger Cove has taught me that."

Her mouth formed a grim line, and then she stepped back onto her boat.

As I made my way up the dock, I reflected on Prudence's warning. It seemed that she too had a sense that the peril wasn't over.

A flash of lightening pierced the sky, followed by a crack of thunder.

I pulled my scarf around my face and shivered—this time for real.

Here comes that storm.

* * *

The rain pounding on the roof of The Clip and Sip break room almost drowned out the cheesy hold music coming from my speakerphone.

I didn't want to do it, but I turned the volume all the way up. As the opening notes of "Crazy Train" played, I cocked a brow. *Ozzy Osborne? What kind of Muzak is this?*

The back door creaked open, and a damp Gia shoved her way inside. She was holding so many shopping bags that she was visible only from her tangerine eye shadow up and from her tiger-striped heels down.

"It's three o'clock," I said, refusing to move a muscle to help her. "What happened to watching the salon while I ran errands this morning?"

"Don't worry," she grunted. "I forwarded the calls to my cell." She let go of her wet load without warning, and the sopping packages tumbled onto me, the table, and the floor.

"Would you please watch what you're doing?" I lifted a soggy bag from my phone. Fortunately, the soothing sounds of Ozzy were still wafting from the speaker.

Gia removed her black lace blazer to reveal a white T-shirt with the phrase "Italian swag" and smirked. "You're not actually listening to that white noise, are you?"

I sighed. "Believe me, I'm trying not to. But I've been on hold with the manufacturer of that syringe for over an hour."

"Are they willing to help you?" she asked, hanging her jacket to dry on the back of a chair.

"So far." I took a sip of my jasmine tea. "Where have you been, anyway?"

She opened the refrigerator and bent over to peer inside. "Fabric shopping."

I blinked. "You can sew?"

"How do you think I got this?" She pointed to the rear of her orange satin A-line midi skirt.

"It's nice," I admitted, examining her backside. "Your skirt, I mean. And thank you for taking off that Devils jersey."

She pulled a DRY rhubarb soda from the fridge and slammed the door. "Well, I didn't do it for you," she said, popping open the can with a white fingernail that said "Fendi." "I had to change my clothes and my nail polish after that garbage escapade."

My eyes narrowed to slits.

Luckily for Gia, the Muzak stopped.

I picked up the phone to make sure that the line hadn't dropped. "Hello?"

"Yes, Miss Conti," a modulated male voice replied. "Sorry about the wait, but I had to search our archives to locate the information you requested."

Gia and I exchanged a puzzled look.

"So," I began, "does that mean the syringe is old?"

"It's from 2005."

"But that doesn't make sense," I protested. "Why would the EMTs here in Danger Cove be using a syringe that's ten years old?"

"It's like I always say," Gia asserted. "Nothing ever happens around here."

I shot her a stare that shut her mouth.

The caller cleared his throat. "I can't speak to why ten-year-old syringes are in use in Danger Cove. But I can tell you that the syringes in the batch number you provided were originally sold to the Presley-Smith Memorial Hospitals in Jackson and Gulfport."

I was so stunned that I was speechless.

Gia slurped her soda like a Japanese diner slurping soup. "So, where are Jackson and Gulfport, anyway?"

"Uh," he began, "that would be Mississippi."

I put my head in my hand. We Contis and our kin weren't exactly worldly. "Is there anything else you can tell me about the syringes?"

"That's all the data I have on this particular batch number," he replied. "Is there anything else I can help you with?"

"That's all. Thank you," I said and then closed the call. "What do you make of that?"

The salon bell buzzed as the door opened.

"I don't know," Gia said, looking into the lobby from her seat. "What do *you* make of *that*?"

I stood up and entered the salon. Detective Ohlsen and Detective Marshall were standing beside the reception desk. "Good afternoon," I said, going to meet them. "Is everything okay?"

Gia came to my side. "This is about Lucy, isn't it?"

"Actually," Detective Ohlsen began, "this is about Dr. Seth Windom."

Somehow I knew that this was the moment I'd been dreading all day.

"Were you aware that he was reported missing yesterday?" he continued.

I gasped. "But I saw him last night!"

Gia elbowed me in the side à la Amy. "What she means is that he was at the Smugglers' Tavern for the Save the Lighthouse Committee fundraiser."

Detective Marshall curled his lips into a sneer. "We're aware of that, miss."

Gia, in turn, curled her fingers into fists. "Then maybe you should be out looking for him."

I took a step forward to prevent a fight with the fuzz, and Detective Ohlsen held up his hand.

"Now everyone stay calm," he said. "We found Dr. Windom."

"That's right," Detective Marshall said as he fixed a cold stare first on Gia and then on me. "And guess where he was?"

"At home?" I offered in a hopeful tone.

"Dead on the rocks below the Smugglers' Tavern," he said through clenched teeth.

Gia gripped my arm, and I covered my mouth.

"That's horrible," I whispered. "I…I can't believe it." I paused to let the terrible reality of another senseless death sink in. And then another terrible reality rained down on me like all of Gia's shopping bags. "But…why are you telling this to me?"

Detective Ohlsen licked his lips. "We found your name in Dr. Windom's patient calendar, and—"

"And," Detective Marshall interrupted, "he was as blue as the regulation shirt on Detective Ohlsen's back."

CHAPTER TEN

A blast of thunder shook the salon as though punctuating the shocking news of Dr. Windom's cerulean skin.

The slight movement of the building was all it took to knock my legs out from under me. I capsized onto the Rococo Revival lobby couch and felt like I was drowning in a sea of blue. It seemed like everywhere I turned I saw the dreadful color—on Margaret Appleby's body, the police uniforms, even the fabric I was sitting on. But why turn Dr. Windom blue too?

Detective Marshall bent over and stared into my eyes. "What happened?" he asked with feigned innocence. "Did that trick knee of yours give out again?"

I descended further into the sofa. Obviously, the police knew the reason for my appointment with Dr. Windom, and they were having none of it. I was officially in hot water, and if they were aware of the break-in too, I was sunk.

With a loud exhale, Detective Ohlsen pinched the bridge of his nose. "Lester," he began in a tired tone, "that's enough."

Emboldened by his reprimand, Gia jutted out her "Italian swag" and clenched and unclenched her fists like she was preparing for a prizefight. "Just what is Barney Fife here trying to imply about my cousin?"

Detective Marshall's eyes narrowed at the Mayberry mockery, and his pecs perked up like Gia's Chicken-Filleted chest. "That she's as phony as your fingernails, Snooki."

"You did *not* just call my nails fake," she fumed, forgetting all about me—and that *Jersey Shore* slight.

Detective Ohlsen's neck turned as crimson as my living room couch. "You two keep this childish behavior up, and I'll put you both in a time out."

A vein protruded from Detective Marshall's forehead, and he spun around and started pacing in the salon like a caged animal.

Gia, in turn, flopped onto the couch beside me, crossed her arms and legs, and began bouncing her tiger-striped foot back and forth like she wanted to kick some cops in the can.

"As for you, young lady," Detective Ohlsen continued, turning to me, "I'd like to know what you were doing at Dr. Windom's office yesterday, and don't tell me that you were there about your knee."

"If I were you, Cass, I'd lawyer up," Gia said from the side of her mouth. "These two have already made up their minds about you."

Detective Ohlsen put his hands on his hips and looked at the ceiling. "I should've listened to my mother and become a fisherman."

Gia held out her hand in protest, purposefully displaying her 100 percent authentic nails—unless you counted that coat of acrylic. "Please. Fishing is a nasty business. If you don't believe me, go take a whiff of that Dumpster out back."

He opened his mouth as if to speak and then seemed to change his mind. Instead, he gestured toward the window overlooking the porch. "Outside," he ordered in a low voice. "And make it snappy."

Gia stood up and stomped her Italian swag to the door, slamming it behind her.

Detective Marshall sneered as he returned to the lobby. "Good rid—"

The last word died on his lips as Detective Ohlsen pointed a finger close to his mouth.

Turning back to me, Detective Ohlsen straightened his collar. "Let me make this clear, Miss Conti. You are not a suspect at this time."

"But she—" Detective Marshall began.

Detective Ohlsen held up a finger again, this time with a wild-eyed look.

Detective Marshall's pumped pecs deflated like a popped inflatable bra insert.

"Now, Miss Conti," he said, running a finger through his hair, "you went to Dr. Windom's office looking for information regarding the death of Margaret Appleby. Is that correct?"

I nodded.

"And you were snooping into the affairs of one Bertha Braun. Am I right?"

I nodded again.

He pursed his lips and clasped his hands behind his back. "I don't think I need to tell you that interfering in a police investigation is a crime. Do I?"

I shook my head.

"And I also don't believe I need to tell you that I will charge you with said crime if I catch you doing anymore meddling. True?"

I started to shake my head but then nodded.

He gave me a pointed look. "I'm glad to see that we're on the same page."

"Yessir, Detective, sir," I croaked. "Me too."

"All right, then," he said as he opened the door. "I'm going to have a word with your cousin in case she should get the urge to do some sleuthing herself." He squinted as though searching my face for signs of Gia's involvement.

I held my breath and focused on staying expressionless, which was no small feat with a six-foot-four, two-hundred-plus-pound cop staring me down.

"We'll be in touch," he announced after what seemed like an hour and exited the salon.

Detective Marshall moved to leave but stopped at the threshold. With a penetrating gaze, he pointed two fingers at his eyes and then at mine. Next, he reinflated his chest, balled his fists, and shouldered his way out of the salon, no doubt with the intent of trying to subdue Gia.

I leaned forward, gasping for air. If he'd lingered much longer I would've turned blue—but preferably purple. Either way, I was relieved that Detective Ohlsen didn't mention the incident at Margaret's house. Because if he had, I would've sung like Tweety Bird, and I would've taken that bad ol' putty tat, Sylvester, a.k.a. Gia, down with me.

What I wanted to know was whether someone had ratted me out to Detective Ohlsen. If they had, the most likely candidate was Dr. Windom's receptionist because she was the one who scheduled his appointments. Although Donna Bocca was certainly a possibility since her name was on the doctor's calendar too. Of course, Bertha also had a reason to turn me in to the police, but I knew it wasn't her. If it had been, she would have told them about the breaking and entering the minute Clyde reported it to her so that she could have me locked up and out of her hair for good.

The real question was, who killed Dr. Windom? To my mind, everything pointed to Bertha. She was with him the night he died, and they were near where his body was found. What I didn't understand was why she would want to kill him when he was trying to help her. Was she getting back at him for firing her in the first place, or was something more sinister going on between them? And what was Clyde's role in all of this?

There was only one thing I knew for certain. Donna knew that I suspected Bertha, thanks to Dr. Windom. So as soon as the police called Donna in for questioning, if they hadn't already, I was a marked woman—as in blue at the bottom of a cliff.

* * *

Gia hung up the salon phone and switched on the pink neon *Closed* sign. "I have awesome news."

"Good, because I could use some," I said as I attached a *Sale* sticker to a bottle of volumizing shampoo on the lobby product display case.

"I just booked a Sweet Sixteen. It's makeup only, but it's for the birthday girl and four of her friends." She gave a festive fist pump.

I reached for a jar of reconstructing conditioner. "What day are they coming?"

Her fist flopped. "Actually," she hedged, "it's at the client's house. She's too afraid to come to the salon."

I dropped the jar onto the shelf. "Well, *that* news just got a lot less awesome."

"You don't have a problem with it, do you?" She clasped her hands in front of her face in a pleading gesture. "Because this is a perfect opportunity to promote my makeup line."

I sighed. "I guess not, but please remember that this is a Sweet Sixteen, not a Sexy Sixteen. I don't want parents coming after me because you vamped those girls out in smoky eyes, false eyelashes, and glitter lip kits."

Gia did a combined eye roll and hair-flip. "You're such a buzz kill."

"No," I said, pointing a tube of intensive shine treatment at her, "I'm a business owner, and I'm already in tons of trouble."

"I'll say," she agreed, gazing out the front window. "Because Amy's on her way up the sidewalk, and the soles of her Hush Puppies are smoking."

Before I had time to look, the salon door burst open.

"Did-you-hear-about-Dr.-Windom?" Amy gushed in a single breath.

"The police have already informed us," I said, trying to remain calm.

"Well," she breathed, propping herself up with her hands on her highs, "you'll never guess who I saw in the back of a squad car when I was leaving work just now."

"Oh lord, who?" I exclaimed, drawing my hands to my mouth. *So much for keeping my cool.*

"Bertha Braun," she replied, her eyes as big around as a sixteen-ounce tub of hydrating hair masque.

Gia took a seat on the couch. "I hate to say this, Cass, but it's probably because of you."

Amy's eyes widened to the size of the thirty-two-ounce tub of that masque. "You turned Bulldog in to the coppers?"

"Not on your life," I said with a shiver.

She held her hands up in surrender. "Don't include me in this. It's your life, not mine."

"Gee," I said, "thanks for the show of support."

Amy took a seat behind the reception desk and kicked up her Hush Puppies. "So, what do you think is going on with this blue business?"

"I don't know," I replied, marking a container of Blue Magic Hair Dress as *Free.* "But I'm afraid that Bertha is setting up Lucy."

Amy grabbed a feather pen from the desk and started fanning herself. "What about Clyde?"

"He's got to be involved in this somehow," Gia said. "Why else would he have been at Margaret's house?"

"Maybe Bertha's the brain, and he's the *braun.*" Amy snorted and slapped her knee. "Get it? 'Brawn' with a *u*?"

"Speaking of brains," Gia began, "any more jokes like that, and I'll brain *you.*"

Amy was so surprised that you could have knocked her over with a feather pen.

"I'm not sure what Clyde's role in all this is," I said, placing a sticker on a packet of three-minute moisturizing mud, "but I'm hoping to figure that out when I have breakfast with Zac tomorrow."

"Breakfast with Zac," Amy repeated in a dreamy voice. "How I'd like to take a bite of his cinnabun."

Gia grimaced. "It's Cinna*bon.*"

Amy rested her head on the back of her chair. "You say *kartòffel*, I say *kàrtoffel.*"

"Huh?" Gia and I said at the same time.

"It's German for 'potato.'" Amy sat up and looked at her watch. "And since we're talking about grub, it's six thirty. Who's up for seafood?"

Gia wrinkled her lips. "I've had enough fish for one day."

I shot Gia a sideways glance. "After hearing about Dr. Windom, I've lost my appetite. And I don't feel like doing anything anyway."

Amy pointed the pen from Gia to me. "You two need to overcome your inner *schweinehundes.*"

"I give up," Gia said in a bored tone. "What's a shvinehoond?"

"A pig-dog," Amy replied.

Gia scrunched up her face. "Okay, sure, I eat *prosciut*, but nobody said anything about eating no *dog.*"

Amy cocked her head from one side to the other like a puppy trying to understand its owner.

"She meant *prosciutto*," I clarified as I knelt to mark down the clarifiers. "You know, cured Italian ham?"

She stared at me, slack jawed. "I just can't follow you guys sometimes."

Gia and I didn't even bother to exchange a look.

"But anyway," Amy continued, "*schweinehund* is the German equivalent of 'couch potato.' So, you need to resist the urge to do nothing. It *is* Saturday night, after all."

"I can't believe I'm going to say this," Gia said, pressing her fingers to her temples. "But in her own weird, wigged out way, Amy's right. We need to get out of this salon."

Even I had to admit that a change of scenery was in order. "All right. But I wish this town had some Tex Mex."

"Or some friggin' Mediterranean food," Gia added.

I rose to my feet and saw a slender figure climbing the porch steps. "Look who's here!"

The door opened, and Lucy stepped inside.

"You're a sight for sore eyes," I said, although in truth I was taken aback by her appearance. She looked like she'd aged ten years in the past twenty-fours hours. "We're on our way out for a bite to eat. Why don't you come with us?"

She shook her head, dislodging a lock of hair from her faded yellow scrunchie. "After six hours of questioning, I'm just not up for it."

"I know something that might change your mind," I said. "Amy, tell her what you told us."

Amy blinked. "About the pig-dog?"

Gia smirked. "About the police."

"Oh, that." Amy smiled. "They brought Bertha Braun down to the station a little while ago."

"Which could mean that you're no longer a suspect," I added.

Lucy looked down and pulled her shoulder bag to her chest. "There's something you should know."

My stomach fell. The last time she uttered that phrase, I found out about her felony. "Would you like to talk in private?"

"I'm sure it'll be in the news soon," she replied, "so you all might as well know."

At that point my stomach went into a full-on free fall.

Lucy slid onto the couch next to Gia. "Ten years ago, my little brother shattered a bone in his ankle, and Dr. Windom operated on it. It was supposed to be a routine procedure, but something went wrong, and my brother has walked with a limp ever since."

I didn't like the turn this story had taken. "What does that have to do with the investigation?"

"My parents sued Dr. Windom for malpractice, and they lost." A single tear rolled down her cheek. "I was only sixteen at the time, and I was super protective of my baby brother." She bowed her head and picked at her chipped nail polish. "So, I went to Dr. Windom's office and told him that one way or another he would pay for what he'd done."

My stomach bottomed out, and it didn't exactly rebound when I saw the concern in Gia's eyes. This was not a good development, but I had to try to reassure Lucy. "Oh, don't worry about that," I said, faking a reassuring tone. "You were just a kid."

"Yeah," Gia said with an exaggerated wave of her hand. "It was such a long time ago too."

"And, lucky for you," Amy began, "Dr. Windom isn't around to tell the police about it."

Before Amy could say another word, I raised a can of Frizz Taming Spray, and she took cover behind the desk.

"No," Lucy admitted, wiping her face with her hand. "But Bertha Braun is around—and like you said, she's at the police station as we speak." She paused. "Even worse…she was in the examining room with Dr. Windom when I threatened him."

* * *

"Remind me never to eat oysters with Amy again," Gia said, staring into the bathroom mirror as she peeled off a false eyelash. "She gets…frisky."

"Well, if you stand any closer," I said, retrieving a jar of salt scrub from the antique cabinet above the pedestal sink, "I'm going to think *you're* getting frisky."

"I'm sorry, but for a brothel bathroom, this is, like, stupid small." She pulled an "Armani" sticker from her cheek. "And if the one in Vinnie's room was reserved for Madame LaSalle, then where did all those girls bathe?"

I applied a layer of the salt mixture onto my face. "They probably used the sinks in their bedrooms."

Gia began removing her eye makeup with a cotton pad. "Then why have this claw-foot tub and the butt bath here?"

"It's called a bidet," I said, working the scrub into my skin. "And why are you asking me? Do I look like a gold rush era prostitute or something?"

"Not with that girl-next-door look you're always rocking." She picked up a clean swab and started on her face. "What does 'bidet' mean, anyway?"

"When I got a quote from Finials and Facades to renovate Uncle Vinnie's bathroom, Alex told me that it was French for 'pony.' Apparently, they called them that because you straddle them like you would when you ride one."

"Well, this pony wasn't the only thing those girls were straddling," she said, tossing a wad of dirty cotton into the trash.

I leaned over the sink and splashed water onto my face and neck. "Can we please change the subject?"

"What?" she asked, throwing her hands into the air. "I was just trying to get your mind off the murders."

"And I appreciate that." I gave my skin a final rinse. "But I can't help it. I'm worried sick about Lucy, and I'm scared for us and the salon."

"Now that you've brought it up, I think we should talk about Lucy."

I straightened and grabbed a hand towel. "Don't tell me that you still think she's involved in this nightmare."

Gia moved in front of the sink and pulled a tube of hydrating mask from the cabinet. "I don't know what I think anymore. I mean, even you have to admit that she's not the sweet, innocent girl that she seems. First we find out about the felony, then the threat against Dr. Windom."

"I'll admit that Lucy is full of surprises," I said, dabbing at my skin with the towel, "but she's not a killer."

Gia looked at me through the reflection in the mirror. "I don't want to think that she is. But she was at the Smugglers' Tavern the night Dr. Windom was killed, and we don't know what she did after we left."

"Look, I saw Bertha with Dr. Windom on the deck, and she was the one who was feuding with him and Margaret, not Lucy. Also, don't forget about Clyde and his connection to Bertha."

"You're probably right." She opened the tube and squirted a generous amount of the blue mask onto her hand.

The flesh practically crawled off my body. "You're seriously going to stand here and use that blue crap right in front of me?"

"It's Cool Blue Calming Mask," she protested. "Am I supposed to throw away everything I own in this color?"

I narrowed my eyes. "How about just the things that turn your skin blue?"

Gia dropped the mask into the trash and washed her hand.

"Anyway," I continued, "I was thinking about it over dinner, and I've decided to give Vinnie's black book to the police."

"How come?" she asked, spreading moisturizer on her face.

"Because I can't shake the feeling that Vinnie's death is related to what's happening now. And if that's the case, then that book could contain something that proves Lucy's innocence."

"Let me make a copy of it first. We might need it for some reason."

"Okay, but you need to do it before I have the officer come to oversee the plumbing work on Monday. I want to be sure to give it to whoever he or she is so that I can steer clear of the police station and Detective Marshall." I turned to leave.

"Wait." She picked up her phone from the vanity. "Before you go to bed, I want you to listen to this."

I looked over her shoulder as she pulled up her music app. "What is it?"

"'Splish Splash.'" She tapped play. "By Bobby Darin."

I paid close attention to the lyrics, hoping to hear something that I could connect to the crimes.

"Can you believe people used to like this music?" She wrinkled her forehead. "It sounds so 1950s."

"Well, duh," I said, giving her a playful shove. "But it's fun."

She smiled and then cast a suspicious glance at her phone. "The crazy thing is that this guy's real name was Walden Robert Cassotto. How do you suppose he went from a fine Italian-American monogram like that to Bobby Darin?"

"Well, Bobby is from Robert, and Darin—" I stopped in midsentence as I finally made the connection.

"What's wrong? You look like you swallowed some of your salt scrub."

I put my hand on my forehead. "The *bd* in Uncle Vinnie's book! It stands for *Bobby Darin.*"

"That doesn't make sense." Gia sat on the side of the bathtub. "The men listed in the book had numbers in the hundreds beside their names. They couldn't be ordering hundreds of Bobby Darin haircuts."

"Right! *Bobby Darin*, or *bd*, is code for something else."

"I see what you mean. Those two calls we got weren't about haircuts—they wanted to place bets."

I shook my head. "Uncle Vinnie wasn't running a betting ring. He was selling something illegal."

"Like what? Drugs?"

"No clue," I replied. "But I'll lay you ten-to-one odds that it had something to do with the color blue."

CHAPTER ELEVEN

"Now *these* are some Seattle Dutch Babies," Zac said, pointing at the fluffy, fruit-topped flapjacks that the server had just delivered.

I cut into mine and took a bite. "Wow," I said, covering my mouth with my hand. "It's like a hybrid between a pancake and a popover."

"Normally they're served with lemon wedges, but since we're at The Apple Tree, they put apples on top." Zac took a big bite of his Baby and looked at his watch.

I glanced at his face as I reached for the syrup. "Do you need to be somewhere soon?"

"Not until eleven. I picked up some extra hours at work today."

In what was undoubtedly a local faux pas, I drowned my Baby in the thick, maple goodness. "Saving to buy back the Pirate's Hook Marine Services?"

"Always," he replied with a curt nod. "But working overtime isn't going to get me my father's company back."

I smiled. "You could always look for the treasure that Bart Coffyn stole from Sir Francis Drake."

He laughed. "I was thinking more along the lines of selling my design for a new sailboat. But if I thought I could find that treasure, I'd be looking for it."

"What does it consist of?" I asked before inhaling a huge hunk of my Baby.

"No one knows." He cradled his steaming cup of Seattle's Best in his hands. "The only thing historians agree on is that Drake and his crew had plundered a Spanish warship and a Spanish galleon called *Nuestra Señora de la Concepción* before sailing the *Golden Hind* up to Washington. The booty is something of a mystery, but there is some evidence that it included silver pesos, gold bullion, pieces of eight, assorted jewels, and pearls. So, Coffyn could've taken any of those things."

"Did your dad have any ideas about what Coffyn took?" I asked, reaching for my apple juice.

He swallowed a sip of coffee. "He was convinced that he'd stolen some of the pesos, because they were the most plentiful and would have been the easiest to carry, and probably some of the more valuable jewels."

"Have you thought about picking up where your father left off? I mean, if you have records of where he searched, you're already ahead of the game."

"If I had proof that the treasure was really out there, I would. And I wouldn't do it for the money, either. I'd do it for my dad."

My eyes welled with tears, and I looked down at what was left of my Baby, which was already surprisingly little. It was hard not to be moved by Zac's devotion to his father, and it was even harder not to be impressed by it. I was starting to think that I'd been a little hasty in writing him off as the superficial type.

"Hey," Zac said in a soft voice. He reached out and tilted my chin upward so that he could look into my eyes.

Not only did I not resist, but I met his gaze straight on. And I let myself get completely lost in the two pools of smoldering blue, so much so that I was ready to rethink my stance on the color—once I started thinking again, that is. Then, out of the corner of my eye, I saw it. The bleached-blonde brigade. Grace, Helen, and Jackie had entered the restaurant, and they were making a beeline for our table.

I stood up and almost knocked over my chair, wanting to be anywhere but at the table with Zac and his legions of women.

He looked up at me with eyes that had lost their smolder and now showed only surprise.

"Excuse me for a moment," I said in a terse tone. "I need to visit the powder room."

"Yoo-hoo, Zac," a high-pitched female voice cried, and a cacophony of giggles followed.

Yoo-hoo? Who says that? I wondered as I headed toward the opposite end of the restaurant, resisting the urge to look back.

I took a left down a narrow hallway and entered the ladies' room. It was a single, so I turned the lock and pressed my back against the door. Then I asked myself a hard question—why had I cut and run on Zac? Of course, it didn't matter one bit to me that his fan club had come to fawn all over him. But didn't the peroxide squad have anything better to do than follow him all over town?

Uh-oh. I knew that last question was a sure sign that I wasn't exactly Switzerland where Zac was concerned, and that wasn't good. After that stunt I'd pulled at the altar, I'd sworn off relationships for a good, long time.

I stole a glimpse of my reflection in the mirror. My face told me what my brain didn't want to acknowledge—that I was upset about the interruption, and it wasn't because I needed to talk to Zac about Clyde. I'd been enjoying hanging out with him and talking to him about his life and his plans. I mean, let's be honest—Gia and Amy weren't what you'd call engaging conversationalists. So why did those fake fair-haired floozies have to ruin it for me?

Nope, not Swiss at all.

This time I turned and stared into the mirror. The truth was as plain as the nose on my face. I was jealous of Grace, Helen, and Jackie—practically green with envy. But I reminded myself that I was here on business, not pleasure. So, I had to suck it up, go back out there, and get the information I needed, bottled blondes or no.

I washed and dried my hands and then checked my attitude in the mirror. And on my way out of the bathroom, I told myself that there was a silver lining to this situation—I was just green, not blue.

As I made my way back to the table, I was relieved to see that the gaggle of girls was gone. But, to my disappointment, Zac's demeanor had changed. He was staring out the window and drumming his fingers on the table, and I noticed that his napkin was in his plate of half-eaten food. Clearly, after meeting up with his groupies, he was ready to move on to bigger and blonder things.

I pulled out my chair and decided to get straight to the point. "I know you have things to do, so I'll make this quick."

Zac started. "Okay?"

"I need you to tell me what you know about Clyde Willard," I said. But instead of looking him in the eyes, I focused on his forehead. It was safer.

His brow creased. "I thought you said you needed to talk to me about The Clip and Sip."

I hated to lie, but I couldn't just blurt out that I suspected Clyde of murdering Margaret. "This *is* about the salon. I'm thinking of hiring him to do some work around the place. And since Gia and I are alone in that house, I need to be sure that he's a good person."

"Right." He toyed with the handle of his coffee cup. "I don't know much about him on a personal level. Clyde doesn't talk a whole lot. But I'm sure he's single, and he said that he lives in a garage apartment somewhere on the edge of town."

I picked up my fork and stabbed my Baby. Zac may have lost his appetite, but I was resolved not to lose mine. "What type of work does he do for the Pirate's Hook Marine Services?"

"Boat repair, odd jobs," he said with a shrug. "Anything we need, basically."

"Is he a hard worker? And honest?" I shoved a supersized bite into my mouth.

He leaned back in his chair and hooked his thumbs into the belt loops of his jeans. "I heard through the rumor mill that someone in town had accused him of stealing a lawn mower. But I've never known him to do anything dishonest."

I looked at my plate and tried to think of other questions that I should ask. This sleuthing thing was so much harder in real life than it seemed in books, especially when the guy you were interrogating could really fill out a pair of pants.

"As for his work ethic," Zac continued, "he's the best boat repairman I've ever worked with, aside from my dad. That's saying a lot, considering that my father had an engineering degree from one of the best universities in the world, and Clyde picked up his skills working offshore in Gulfport."

I dropped my fork like it had scalded my hand. "Did you say 'Gulfport'—as in, Mississippi?"

"Yeah, according to his résumé, he worked for the oil industry there until a decade or so ago."

So Clyde had lived in one of the cities where the syringe had been sold at around the time the Presley-Smith Memorial Hospital would have purchased it. Was this it? Was Clyde the murderer?

Zac leaned across the table. "Cassidi, are you all right?"

As soon as he asked me the question, a cold, clammy sensation came over me—not for myself, but for Gia. She was still sleeping when I'd left, and she was alone in that huge house.

"Could you please take me home?" I asked, leaping to my feet. "Like, as fast as you can get me there."

* * *

Zac pulled his Jeep in front of The Clip and Sip and switched off the engine.

I took one look at the place and knew that something was wrong. And it wasn't even because the front door was wide open. It was the way that the *Closed* sign was hanging by one end.

"Oh no," I breathed. I threw open the door and jumped from the car.

"Cassidi, wait," Zac called as I ran toward the porch. "Don't go inside."

Ignoring his command, I took the steps two at a time and stopped short in the doorway.

The salon had been ransacked. Most of the products I'd marked down the day before lay scattered and broken on the floor, and the reception desk drawers had been pulled out and emptied. The hair-cutting stations had met a similar fate.

Tears stung the backs of my eyes, and when I felt Zac's strong arms wrap around me, I succumbed to his embrace. And for a moment, all was forgotten.

"Why don't you wait outside?" he whispered, stroking my hair. "I'll call the police."

As much as I didn't want to, I pulled away. "Gia could be upstairs. I have to make sure that she's all right."

"I'll go." He pulled his phone from his pocket and called 9-1-1. "You go out to the porch and wait for the police."

"I'm going with you," I replied.

Zac held up a hand to silence me. "Yes, I'd like to report a break-in at The Clip and Sip Hair Salon."

I headed for the stairs.

"Cassidi!" he yelled.

I ran up the spiral staircase and bolted down the hall. Glancing into my room, I saw that my dresser drawers and closet had all been emptied. I turned toward Gia's room and grasped the door handle.

It wouldn't open.

"The police are on their way," Zac said from behind me.

I looked at him with panic. "Gia's room is locked."

"Move out of the way."

I stepped back, and he rammed the door open with his shoulder.

Gia was on the bed with her arms and legs splayed. She had a mask over her eyes, and her mouth was hanging open.

If I didn't know better, I would have said that she was practicing the yoga posture, shavasana, or death pose.

"Call an ambulance," Zac said, tossing me his phone as he ran to Gia's side.

I caught the phone between my trembling hands. "No, that's just how she—"

"Back off, bro!" Gia barked as she flew from the bed in her Wonder Woman pajamas, ripping the gold and red-starred headband from her eyes on the way. She swung a baseball bat that she'd produced out of nowhere. "Or I'm gonna go all Jersey on you."

"—sleeps," I said, sinking into the beanbag chair.

Gia flipped her red, white, and blue cape and then her black hair. "You might be a hottie, Zac Taylor, but that doesn't give you the right to enter into a lady's room uninvited."

I had to cock a brow at the "lady" part.

Zac held his hands high, as though facing an entire SWAT unit. "I was just making sure that you were okay."

"Lower your club, Lynda Carter," I said with a surly stare. "The salon and my bedroom were broken into while you were getting your superhero sleep. Zac is trying to help us."

The bat clattered to the floor. "OMG. It had to be Clyde. You *know* he saw you—"

I made a slicing motion across my neck at the same time Zac tilted his head.

"Would one of you mind telling me what's going on here?" he asked, crossing his arms against his chest.

Gia looked at me, and I looked at Zac.

I couldn't tell him that we'd seen Clyde searching Margaret's house. It's not that I thought that he would report us, but I knew that he would think badly of me, and I realized that I didn't want him to. "I think Clyde might have had something to do with Margaret Appleby's murder and with Dr. Windom's as well."

Zac's arms fell to his sides. "That's an awfully serious accusation. Do you have any proof?"

Even before he'd uttered the word, I realized why someone had torn through my salon and my room. I rolled from the beanbag and sprung to my feet. When I arrived at my nightstand, I saw the top drawer lying empty on the floor.

I sunk onto the side of the bed and put my face into my hands. "It's all gone," I said. "The syringe wrapper, the Bible. And I have no proof that any of it ever existed."

Gia slipped her arm around my shoulders. "You don't need it, Cass. I saw those things, and Amy did too. The police will believe that."

I turned my head to look at her. "Yes, but they won't be able to prove it in court."

"What's this about a syringe wrapper and a Bible?" Zac asked from the doorway.

"Nothing," Gia intoned and waved him away.

Zac's face grew dark. "I'll go downstairs to wait for the police."

Gia nodded at him.

The disappointment in Zac's voice stayed with me after he'd left the room. But no one was more disappointed in me than me. What had I been thinking, trying to solve a murder investigation on my own? Thanks to my inexperience, we'd not only lost evidence tying the killer to Margaret's death, but now we would never know what the babies in that Bible had to do with the crime.

Gia pulled my hair onto my back. "What's on your mind?"

"Those babies listed in the Bible," I replied, resting my elbows on my knees. "And no matter how I look at it, I just keep coming back to the same thing."

"What's that?" She reached for a tube of raspberry lotion that had been knocked from the nightstand.

"They had to be babies that Margaret delivered."

"That makes sense to me," she said, smoothing lotion on her arms. "But how can we prove it now that we don't have their names?"

"I know!" I sat up. "We start by calling the Presley-Smith Memorial Hospitals in Gulfport and Jackson."

"What?" She tossed the tube back onto the floor. "Why would we do that?"

"Because we know that the syringe came from one of those places and because I found out from Zac that Clyde used to work in Gulfport."

"Whoa." She gripped her star-spangled thighs. "So, Clyde is the killer!"

I shook my head. "Not necessarily. But it's looking more and more like something happened down in Mississippi. And if we can trace Bertha or even Margaret to one of those hospitals, then we're on our way to finding out what that was."

"You know that Human Resources won't just give out information to anyone who calls. They'll probably ask for a signed release."

"You're industrious. You'll think of something."

"Me?" She put a hand to her W-emblazoned chest. "Why can't *you* call the hospitals?"

I stood up and looked out the window in front of my desk. "Because the police will be here any minute, and I'll be going down to the station with them. I think it's time to tell them about Clyde."

"Wait." She held up a hand. "You're not going to tell them about us breaking into Margaret's, are you? Because we'll get arrested." She gestured to her heroic form. "And you know that this isn't suited to life in the pen."

"Relax, Wonder Woman," I said, glowering at her from the corner of my eyes. "As much as I'd like to throw you under the bus sometimes—and by that I also mean under a large, oncoming vehicle—I have no plans to do so right now." I glanced around my disheveled room. "In fact, apart from asking them to send an officer to oversee the plumber tomorrow morning, I don't have the faintest idea what I'm going to say."

A police siren wailed in the distance.

But from the sound of things, I'd better think of something quick.

* * *

Detective Marshall shined the hanging metal lamp into my eyes. "Let's try this again," he said, his face so close that I could smell the doughnut burger that he'd just eaten for lunch. "Exactly how did you come into possession of the syringe wrapper?"

By this point I was so frustrated that I wanted to scream. "Like I said," I began, trying to control my temper, "I found it in the flowerbed outside the salon. Now can I please speak to Detective Ohlsen?"

He smirked and released the light. "Oh you'd like that, wouldn't you? Because you've pegged him for a sucker," he said, pulling up his pants. "For you he's just another man who you can twist around your finger."

I glanced at the time on my phone. I hadn't seen Detective Ohlsen since he'd driven me from the salon to the station four hours before, and I was getting worried that he wasn't coming back. Because judging from the way things were going, Detective Marshall was going to have me locked up *and* prosecuted within the hour.

"So now you're speechless, huh?" He snorted and pointed his finger at me. "Well, I know your type, all right. You're just like your uncle—always on the make." He placed his hands on the table and leaned toward me. "Tell me, did Vinnie tip you off to Margaret Appleby's money before his, uh, unfortunate demise? Or did you sniff out her dough all by your little lonesome?"

I squirmed in my seat. I'd been under the impression that the focus of the investigation had shifted from Lucy to Bertha, but it was starting to seem like it had actually shifted to me.

The door opened, and Detective Ohlsen appeared in the threshold. "I'll take it from here, Lester."

I breathed an audible sigh of relief.

Detective Marshall's ruddy complexion got even ruddier. Then he leveled a glare at me.

I was tempted to stick my tongue out at him, but I didn't dare. He'd slap me with an assault charge faster than you could say "freeze."

Detective Ohlsen cleared his throat, and Detective Marshall turned and stormed from the room like a linebacker for the Dallas Cowboys.

"Would you like something to drink?" Detective Ohlsen asked as he placed his coffee cup and a folder on the table.

If anything, I wanted something to eat. I'd been in this interrogation room for so long that my Dutch Baby had grown up and left home. "No thank you, Detective. What I'd really like is to know whether or not I'm under arrest."

He took a seat in the folding chair and pulled a pair of bifocals and a pen from his shirt pocket. "That depends." He slipped on his glasses and began writing on a sheet of paper inside the folder. "If I decide that you interfered with the investigation, yes. Otherwise, I'll see to it that you're released."

I began fiddling with a ring on my finger. "I already told you that I meant to give you the syringe wrapper, but it was stolen before I could."

"And I told you that if you hadn't waited to call the manufacturer, you wouldn't be sitting here right now."

"But I wanted to be sure that the wrapper was pertinent to the case."

He stopped writing and stared at me over the rim of his bifocals. "That's for us to investigate, young lady."

"Yessir, Detective." I mustered all the sincerity I could manage and added, "I'm really sorry that I didn't turn it in as soon as I found it. I mean, I know it will be harder to catch the killer without it."

He removed his glasses and laid them on the table. "In most cases, a stunt like the one you pulled could allow a killer to go free."

I hung my head. He was right, and I felt terrible about it. The last thing I wanted was for someone like Bertha or Clyde to be on the loose.

"But fortunately for you," he continued, closing the folder, "we don't need that wrapper."

My head snapped up. "You don't?"

He shook his head. "We located the syringes in question this morning."

I couldn't have been more stunned than if he'd hit me upside the head with Gia's baseball bat. "So—"

"So," he interrupted, "we caught the killer." He slipped his pen and his glasses back into his pocket. "I just arrested your employee Lucy O'Connell for the murders of Margaret Appleby and Seth Windom."

CHAPTER TWELVE

"But...how can that be?" I would have expected this decision from Detective Marshall but not Detective Ohlsen. "Lucy's innocent. You have to know that."

Detective Ohlsen looked down at the table and toyed with his bifocals. "I don't like it any more than you do, Miss Conti. But the evidence points to Miss O'Connell."

"What about Clyde?" I asked, hoping to convince him to reconsider his position. "I told you that he worked in Gulfport at around the same time that the syringe might have been shipped there."

"There are two issues with that sentence." He held up his index finger. "First, 'at around the same time.' And second," he said as his middle finger shot up, "'might have been.'" He put his hands flat on the table, as though bracing for a storm. "Now, you and I both know that a whole lot of people have worked in Gulfport at one time or another, and from the sound of things, there was never any proof that the syringe made it there or to Jackson, for that matter."

When he put it that way, my theory did sound weak. But I refused to believe that Lucy had committed these crimes. "Can you at least tell me where the syringes were found?"

He gave a slow, distracted nod, like someone recalling an unpleasant memory. "They were buried beneath Miss O'Connell's bedroom window."

My mind flashed to the prescription pad I'd found planted in my trash, but I knew better than to mention that not-so-insignificant detail to Detective Ohlsen. "That doesn't mean anything," I said. "Anyone could have buried them there. Like

Clyde. I heard that he's been seen peeping into women's windows."

Detective Ohlsen's brow knotted. "You be careful, young lady." He pointed his bifocals at me. "You're accusing Mr. Willard of some serious infractions that you don't have a shred of evidence to back up."

I looked at my lap. He was right—I couldn't prove the voyeurism accusations any more than I could the syringe connection. I wished that I could come clean about seeing Clyde in Margaret's house, but if Detective Ohlsen knew the full extent of my investigation, he'd lock me up for sure. And I couldn't let that happen, because Lucy needed me now more than ever. The only thing I could do was to try to plant a seed of doubt in his mind about her guilt. "Are you positive that the syringes are associated with the murders?"

"Both of them contained trace amounts of a blue substance," he replied in a matter-of-fact tone.

I leaned forward in my chair, anxious to find out whether I'd been right about the murder weapon. "Was it the hair dye?"

His jaw tensed, as though it regretted what he was about to say. "Actually, the lab identified the substance as Barbicide."

I did my best to look surprised, which wasn't hard, considering that I hadn't really been expecting to be right. "Well, this changes things, doesn't it?" I asked with a Gia-style gesture. "I mean, hair dye is used in salons, but Barbicide is used in lots of other businesses, like spas and even hospitals."

"True," he said. "But Barbicide was in plain sight on three of the stations at The Clip and Sip, so we have no reason to believe that the Barbicide used in the homicides came from an outside source."

"Okay," I said with a nod. "Let's say the Barbicide *did* come from my salon, which it probably did. Then tell me what motive would Lucy have had to kill my Uncle Vinnie?"

A wrinkle appeared on Detective Ohlsen's brow. "I'm not sure I follow you. We have no evidence to indicate that Vinnie's death is related to Margaret's."

"Maybe not. But you have to admit that it's awfully coincidental that two people were murdered in the same hair salon."

There was a knock at the door, and a fiftyish-looking officer with a Magnum PI mustache peered into the room. "Can I see you for a moment, Bud?"

"Sure." Detective Ohlsen rose to his feet. "You stay put, Miss Conti."

I watched him leave with a feeling of dread in the pit of my stomach. At this point, I'd run out of ways to try to poke holes into Detective Ohlsen's case against Lucy. And since he didn't believe that Clyde was involved, my only option was to find some way to connect Bertha to the crimes. But first, I wanted to talk to Lucy.

Detective Ohlsen returned, his expression drawn.

"Can I see Lucy?" I blurted out, sensing that all was not well with my friend.

He shook his head. "I'm afraid that's not possible," he replied, reaching for the file. "I've just learned that she's been taken to urgent care."

* * *

Gia placed the salon phone receiver on the cradle and returned to her station. "Lucy was having chest pains, but her mom said it was just stress."

"I can imagine, with the charges she's facing," I said as I straightened the overturned shampoos surrounding the sink at my station. "We have to do something to help her. Otherwise, they're going to try her for two counts of murder. Maybe three if they can tie Uncle Vinnie's death into this awful mess."

"And all because of that *mamaluke*, Detective Marshall," Gia said as she knelt to retrieve her makeup brushes from the floor.

Amy stopped sweeping and rested both hands on the broom handle. "He's descended from the Turkish Mamelukes? I thought *Marshall* was Frankish."

"I don't know what *mamaluke* means in Turkey," Gia began with a brow raise, "but where I come from, it means *fool*." She gave Amy a pointed look.

"Actually, Detective Marshall didn't arrest her," I said, lining up the conditioners. "It was Detective Ohlsen."

"What?" Gia threw a batch of brushes into a drawer for emphasis. "I thought he was the good one."

"He is the good one," I replied. "He let me go today when he should've thrown the book at me." I glanced at the undisturbed jar of Barbicide on Lucy's station. "And besides, he didn't seem happy about arresting Lucy. The problem is that the evidence implicates her."

"Then it sounds like you need to find new evidence," Amy said, sweeping the shards of a jar of molding wax into a pile.

"Easier said than done." I pulled an intact tube of Dye Hard Hair Color Styling Gel from beneath my chair and threw it in the trash. It was red, not blue. But still. "That reminds me, Gia, did you call the hospitals?"

"Their HR offices are closed on Sundays." She inserted a tube of lipstick into a display case. "I'll do it first thing tomorrow."

"With any luck, they'll be able to help us trace Bertha and Margaret to Mississippi." I sat in my salon chair. "If not, I don't know what we're going to do."

Amy emptied her dustpan. "Why don't you talk to Santiago Beltrán?"

Gia looked at Amy like she'd never seen her before. "That's a good idea, Cass. He might be able to tell you whether Bertha's ever lived in Gulfport or Jackson."

"Come to think of it," I said tilting my head, "I know where to find him too. Dee Madison mentioned that he lives at the Coveside Retirement Resort."

"Resort?" Gia snorted. "Who do they think they're kidding?"

"The elderly," Amy replied as serious as a pacemaker.

A knocking sound came from the entrance.

Gia turned toward the salon door. "It's a couple of older ladies. Hopefully, they're here to update their hairstyles."

"I'll go see what they want," I said, pushing myself from the chair.

As I made my way to the lobby, the sixty-something women—one with a bouffant bob, the other with a fifties flip—cheered me on with encouraging smiles.

"Pardon us for intruding," bouffant bob said the second I opened the door. "I'm Eve Hazlitt, and this is Loretta Tupper." She gestured toward fifties flip. "We know you're not usually open on Sundays, but our husbands surprised us with tickets to see a play in Seattle at seven o'clock tonight, so we were hoping you'd accept two walk-ins."

I hated to let them see the salon in its current state, but I couldn't refuse the business. "That should give me plenty of time to style your hair."

"Oh, we're not here for our hair," Loretta said, fluffing her flip. "We need our faces done."

Gia arrived at the door so quickly that I would've sworn she'd flown in on Amy's broom.

"We saw what you did with Bertha Braun's makeup," Loretta continued as wide-eyed as Betty Boop, "and it was exactly what we're looking for."

Gia shot me a triumphant look and then flashed an Academy Award winner's smile. "That was me," she gushed. "And thank you."

"Since we're going to see *Wicked*, we want that same witchy look," Eve said as innocent as her Garden of Eden namesake.

I saw Gia's triumphant look and raised her a righteous one. "Most definitely."

Loretta flipped her flip. "With my fair coloring, I'm more Glinda. But with Eve's dark hair and olive skin, she's obviously Elphaba."

"I agree completely," I said, tickled pink. "And you've come to the right place because my cousin can work magic with green."

Gia cast me a look as black as a cauldron. "Would you ladies please follow me?"

I stepped aside to allow the women to enter.

"And Cassidi," Gia began in a Wicked-Witch-of-the-West tone, "could you get to work straightening up the lobby? This mess is a hazard for our clients."

I deserved that. But it so was worth it.

Amy entered the lobby. "What should I do next?"

"I've got this," I said, looking around at the disarray. "Why don't you see what you can do with the break room?"

"*Wunderbar*," Amy said, and then she skipped to the back of the salon.

I rolled my eyes and my sleeves and set about salvaging salon products.

I'd put a grand total of one item on the shelf when my phone began to vibrate. I pulled it from my pocket and looked at the display, but I didn't recognize the number. "Hello?"

"Hi, Cassidi. It's Zac."

"Oh," I exclaimed, not so much because I was surprised that he'd called but because I was surprised that my heart had skipped a beat.

"I was calling to find out whether you'd made it back from the police station." He paused. "And to ask if you wanted me to stay there tonight."

So, we have breakfast together, and then this? Maybe I wasn't wrong about him being a player. "I'm sorry," I said with an icy edge. "What did you just say?"

He cleared his throat. "I meant that I'd sleep in The Clip and Sip. You know, to keep an eye on things."

Either Zac didn't know that Lucy had been arrested, or he didn't think that she was the killer. Whatever the reason, I was touched by his offer—now that I knew he wasn't up to no good, of course. "I appreciate the thought, but we'll be all right. I mean, whoever ransacked the place got what they came for. And besides, Gia does have her Wonder Woman superpowers."

He gave an I'm-glad-we're-good-again chuckle. "Don't forget the bat."

"How could I?" I giggled at the memory of Zac with his hands up. "So you see—we're well protected."

He was silent for a moment. "Well," he began in a low voice, "if you change your mind, you know I'll be there."

My heart swelled. "Thank you. I—"

A woman gave a throaty laugh on the other end of the line. "Oh, Zac. That's adorable!"

And then my heart shriveled—to two sizes too small. "—won't be needing your services."

"Cassidi, wait—"

I closed the call and turned off my phone. It was the next best thing to slamming down the receiver. Was Zac Taylor ever without a woman?

I picked up a package of hair extensions and was tempted to strangle someone with it. But I knew that I needed to get a grip and get back to work. After all, it wasn't my business that Zac spent his free time with. I just wished he wouldn't call me when he was with the woman—or women. *The jerk.*

With a sigh, I tossed the extensions into the trash and began restocking the display case.

"Did you hear about Verna's granddaughter, Nancy?" the voice of Eve asked.

I looked into the salon and saw Eve sitting in the empty salon chair next to Gia's station, where Gia was applying a shimmering blue shadow to Loretta's eyes.

"Isn't she the one who's adopting the baby from overseas?" Loretta asked, careful to move only her mouth.

Eve looked into the mirror and gave a bump to her bob. "Not anymore she's not."

Gia turned and looked at Eve. "What happened?"

I quickly placed a tube of hair fattener on the top shelf so that Gia wouldn't notice me eavesdropping. I knew it was impolite, but I was drawn to the conversation for reasons I couldn't explain.

"The country banned international adoptions," Eve replied. "But only after Nancy and her husband had already met the little girl."

Loretta gasped without moving a facial muscle. "Why would they do something awful like that when those poor children need loving homes?"

Eve shrugged and opened a hair magazine. "Apparently, some of the agencies operating in the area are illegally buying babies and then adopting them to US couples."

"Oh my word," Loretta said. "Can you imagine selling children to make a profit?"

The power of her words hit me with such force that I sunk to my knees on the floor. Now I knew why Margaret had hidden her Bible.

Something illegal had happened with those babies listed on the inside flap, and I had the sickening feeling that it had to do with black-market adoption.

* * *

Amy produced the torch lighter that she carried in her satchel in case of emergency, and she lit both of her homemade candles with a flourish.

The scent of pine was immediately so overpowering that it smelled like I was standing in the forest behind my salon rather than in the library. "Wow, those candles have quite an aroma. Are you sure we can't just turn on the lights?"

"They're pungent because I used a steam distillation technique to extract the oil from the pine needles," she said as she opened the drawer of a metal cabinet and began thumbing through the microfiche. "And I already told you. Library employees are not allowed in the building after hours under any circumstances, and Ben goes over the electric bill with a fine-tooth comb. He'll get suspicious if he sees an increase in our kilowatt-hour usage."

I buried my nose in my scarf. "Won't he know that someone was here anyway when he comes in tomorrow morning and the whole place smells like a Christmas tree lot?"

"*Nein.*" She slammed the drawer shut. "The cleaning crew gets here before he does, and they use Pine-Sol on the floors. Hence the pine-scented candles."

"Good thinking," I said. "I guess." I sat down at a microfiche reader, but I didn't dare turn it on until I got the green light from Amy. She didn't like people who wasted electricity anymore than her boss did. And judging from the way she'd brandished that torch lighter, I figured I'd do well to sit tight and wait for her instructions.

Amy took a seat at the machine next to me. "Since Margaret moved to Danger Cove in the mid-eighties, I thought we'd start with 1985 and work forward a few years. If nothing turns up, we'll go backward."

"Sounds like a plan. I'll take Gulfport. You take Jackson."

She handed me a stack of microfiche labeled *Sun Herald* and then loaded her reader with the *Clarion-Ledger*.

We switched on our machines and fell silent as we began the work of sifting through the daily newspapers for anything having to do with illegal adoption. Amy flew through the film at the speed of light, whereas I floundered along at the speed of darkness.

After what seemed like an eternity, I finished my first microfiche and returned it to its envelope. "Talk about dry reading. Studying accounting was more stimulating than this."

"Hey, you haven't mentioned accounting lately," Amy said as she inserted a new microfiche into her reader. "How's that going?"

With everything that had been going on, I'd forgotten all about the class. "I'm glad you brought that up. I need to go online and drop the course before the final exam."

"Why would you do that?" she asked, scrolling through a newspaper. "Isn't the final coming up?"

"It's at the end of the month." I inserted a microfiche into the reader.

Her eyes shot to their corners. "That's tomorrow, you know."

"What?" I leaned over and tugged my daily planner from my purse. I rifled through the unused pages until I got to September and saw that it was indeed the 29th. "So much for organization," I said, shoving my planner back into my bag. "What am I going to do now? It's too late to drop."

She shrugged. "Take the exam."

"But what would be the point?" I exclaimed, not without a note of hysteria. "I made a 50 on the last quiz, which means I have, like, a 58 average."

"Then you could still pass," she said with the calm of a candlemaker. "All you need is a 60."

I crossed my arms. "Maybe if I had your brain."

She gave a combined head wave and eye roll. "It's accounting. Nobody does well on those exams, which is why they're always graded on a curve."

"I'm sure clients of accountants everywhere would be thrilled to hear that."

"Just pull an all-nighter tonight," she said, reaching for another microfiche, "and you'll be fine."

I wasn't anywhere near as confident about that, but she had a point. I had nothing to lose by taking the exam and everything to gain. "Okay, but it's already eight thirty," I said with a nervous glance at the clock. "We'd better get a move on."

Amy pushed up her glasses and leaned closer to her screen. "*Ach mein Gott*!"

I touched her back. "Are you okay?"

She pulled away as though I'd just lit the torch lighter in her face. "Of course. Why do you ask?"

My arm fell to my side. "You made a gagging noise, so I thought you were choking."

"I said 'Oh my God' in German because I think I found something."

"That explains it." I slid my chair closer to hers and looked at the screen. "What did you find?"

"Listen to this. It's from February 15, 1986." She cleared her throat. "'The woman whose newborn was falsely declared deceased and then placed for illegal adoption last year has decided to press charges against Presley-Smith Memorial Hospital after the disappearance of the hospital staff members allegedly involved in the scandal. Doctor Jonas Thorpe and Nurse Leona Hawthorne, who were charged with kidnapping and abduction in the case, are presumed to have fled Jackson to avoid prosecution.'"

I looked at her open mouthed. "The nurse's name was Leona," I whispered. "That's the same name Clyde said in Margaret's house."

Amy's lips formed a grim line. "Do you think there's a connection?"

"I don't know," I said, resting my elbows on my lap. "I guess Leona could have been someone Margaret knew, like a friend or a relative."

"Well, who did the Bible belong to?"

I pressed my temples and tried to focus. "I thought that it was Margaret's. But now that you mention it, I don't remember seeing her name inside, so maybe it belonged to Leona. What else does the article say?"

She turned to the screen. "'Jackson native Hazel Kirkpatrick—'"

I gasped. "Stop right there," I said, leaping to my feet. "I remember that name. There was a 'Baby Kirkpatrick' listed in the Bible."

"So there is a connection," she said.

"It sure looks that way, doesn't it?" I began pacing back and forth in front of the stacks. "Does the article name any other victims?"

She shook her head. "It says that even though Ms. Kirkpatrick got her baby back, she felt that she had a 'personal and moral obligation' to file suit in case other women and their infants were victimized by the hospital staff."

I thought of the thirty babies named in that Bible. "So, no one knew of any other victims in 1986."

"Apparently not." She turned off both of the readers. "Let's go google this case to see what else we can find out."

I followed Amy to the public computers located next to the microfiche readers. She pressed the spacebar to wake the computer from sleep mode and entered both the doctor's and the nurse's names. "Here's an article that explains how Dr. Thorpe and Nurse Hawthorne tricked Ms. Kirkpatrick."

I looked over her shoulder.

She pointed to a line of text. "It says here that they took the baby while she was under anesthesia for an emergency C-section. Then when she woke up they told her it was stillborn."

I rose to my feet and rested a hand on my nauseated stomach. "What awful, horrible people."

"You can say that again." She clicked Images at the top of the screen. "Let's see what these monsters look like."

I leaned forward to scrutinize their photographs and then promptly leaned back. I didn't recognize the doctor, but I knew the nurse.

She was a fifty-something Margaret Appleby.

CHAPTER THIRTEEN

With my head propped on my hands, I watched from the break room table as my third double espresso of the morning dribbled from the machine. The steady stream of liquid had a soothing, hypnotic effect, and my eyelids lowered to a close.

"Well?" Gia's voice punched through the silence like a fist pump.

My eyelids jerked open. Then I jumped.

She stood before me in a black T-shirt, with a giant, gold Medusa on the front, and a pair of black tights. To complete the look, she'd accessorized with a snake-coil bracelet and done her hair in tight ringlet curls that looked a lot like the snakes on Medusa's head. "Did you finish the exam?"

"Not in what I'd call spectacular style," I replied as I tried to rub the scary sight from my eyes. "But I submitted my answers, yes."

"At least it's over." She pulled a newspaper from under her arm and threw it on the table.

"Yeah." I yanked down my Pink sweatshirt as I rose from the table to get my caffeine. "Because now I can get back to focusing on the fun stuff, i.e., the murders, Lucy's incarceration, and the impending failure of my business."

Gia grabbed a bag of bagels and a jar of Nutella from the cabinet and flopped down at the table. "You're in a mood."

"Actually, I feel just like the image on your shirt looks."

She arched a gold-glittered brow. "If you felt like Donatella Versace, *cug*, you'd feel frighteningly fabulous."

I didn't bother to correct her about the identity of the image, because the designer did bear a resemblance to Medusa. "You got the 'frighteningly' part right, because I am afraid." I poured a liberal dose of sugar into my cup. "As soon as I tell Detective Ohlsen about Margaret's double identity, he's going to arrest me for sure."

"So rude," she exclaimed, using her finger to extract a glob of the chocolate-hazelnut spread from the jar. "I mean, he should be thanking you for helping him solve his case."

I slid into my seat. "You know he's not going to see it that way."

"Then don't tell him about Margaret. He keeps telling you that it's his job to do the investigating, so let him do it. What's the worst that could happen?"

"I'll tell you." I leaned forward to make sure she paid attention to me and not the Nutella—which even I had to admit was delightfully distracting. "Someone else could turn up blue, like you or me, for instance."

"Not likely." She calmly licked the chocolaty goo from her fingernail, revealing the Versace Greek key logo. "We don't have anything to do with this adoption vendetta. And besides, how many other people in Danger Cove could possibly be connected to crimes that went down in Mississippi thirty-something years ago?"

I chewed my thumbnail. "What if it's not about the adoptions?"

She gave me a get-real glare. "The woman stole thirty babies from their mothers. It had something to do with her death."

My gut told me that Gia was right, but it was also telling me that there was more to this crime than we suspected—and that I'd had too much espresso. "I'm not sure it's that simple."

"What do you mean?" She spooned chocolate-hazelnut spread onto her bagel.

"Don't forget that Uncle Vinnie died in this building too."

She shook her snakes. "Vinnie couldn't have had anything to do with the illegal adoptions. He lived in Jersey then."

"Well, I think there's a connection between him and Margaret. I just don't know what it is yet."

"Oh, I know what it is." She bit into her bagel with gusto. "A looove connection."

I gave her a stop-it stare and shot the rest of my espresso.

Gia opened the newspaper and then closed it. She had that *I did not just see what I thought I saw* look on her face.

I put my coffee cup on the table for fear that I might launch it. "What is it now?"

"Duncan strikes again."

I reached for the paper and opened it to the front page. The headline "Homicide by Barbicide!" covered the top, and below it the faces of Margaret and Seth were juxtaposed over a photo of the salon. Thankfully, they were not only alive in the image, but they were also in black and white. I pushed the paper away. "At least he didn't use the picture of Sadie again."

"Aren't you going to read it?" she asked with wide, heavily eye-lined eyes.

I stood up and took my coffee cup to the sink. "I have something I need to do right now."

She dropped the bagel onto her plate. "Don't tell me you're going to turn yourself in?"

"Not yet. I want one last shot at tying Bertha to this case."

"About that," she said, resting her forearms on the table. "While you were taking your exam, I called Presley-Smith Memorial, and they have no record of her."

I sunk back into my chair. "Are you sure? Maybe it's HR policy to tell that to callers who don't have a signed release."

"Hey, this is me we're talking about," Gia said with a gesture to her chest that caused the rhinestone eyes on her snake-coil bracelet to flash. "I sent a signed release—signed on behalf of Bertha by me. And the man I spoke to said that Bertha had never worked at that hospital."

I crossed my arms. "Maybe she's using an assumed name, like Margaret was."

"If that were the case, those two wouldn't have peacefully coexisted here in Danger Cove until now."

Gia had a point. If Bulldog had an old bone to pick with Margaret, it would have come out long before now. "You don't suppose that Bertha was one of the mothers whose babies were stolen, do you?"

She gave me a blank look not unlike that of the Medusa on her shirt. "Uh, she would have been something like fifty back then."

"Right. So that's out." I drummed my fingers on the table. "The only other thing I can think of is that she was a relative of one of the women whose babies were stolen."

"That's a long shot."

"Nevertheless, I'm going to talk to Santiago." I stood up and pulled the car keys from my purse. "I have to find out why the police released Bertha and arrested Lucy instead."

"What about the plumber?" She glanced at the clock. "He said he'd be here by nine, which is in fifteen minutes."

"You'll be here to let him in." I opened the door and then turned to face her. "Just call me if it's going to cost more than three hundred dollars, because I might want to get a second bid."

"All right. But be careful, will ya?" She put her hand on Medusa's face. "All of a sudden, I'm getting that bad feeling about today."

"You're such a drama queen," I said and then closed the door behind me. I didn't want to let on, but the truth was that I was getting a bad feeling too.

* * *

"Mr. Beltrán will see you now," a smoky female voice announced.

I looked up from my complimentary plate of salmon-dill-cream-cheese finger sandwiches to see a statuesque, red-saronged brunette with a Coveside Retirement Resort name tag that said *Minka*.

Before we could make eye contact, she turned runway-style and glided down a sparkling marble-floored hallway with gilded paneling.

I shoved a sandwich into my mouth and hurried after her. Judging from what I'd seen of the so-called "resort," the joke was on those of us who didn't live here, not on the elderly. The place was a cross between a luxury condo complex and a spa with a splash of tropical island hotel. It made my old Victorian house look like a rundown, well, brothel.

Minka opened a door and ushered me inside.

What I saw stopped me cold in my tracks, and I stress "cold."

Santiago was lying half-naked and face down—getting a full body massage.

I'd imagined that he'd be wearing linen, as in a Guayabera shirt, but not as in a bedsheet. I looked at the red-muumuued masseuse, whose name tag read *Helga* but could easily have read *Hulk*, and pointed behind me toward the door. "Maybe I should wait outside."

Santiago propped himself onto his forearms. With his thick, white hair and matching mustache, he looked more like Cesar Romero than Ricardo Montalbán. "*Señorita* Conti," he began with a mild accent, "to what do I owe the pleasure?"

I didn't know what made me more uneasy—his fur-pelted back or his emphasis on the word *pleasure.* "Mr. Beltrán, I—"

"Santiago, *por favor.*" He flashed a celebrity smile.

His white dentures contrasted so sharply with his coffee-colored skin that I flinched. "I was hoping to talk to you about the investigation into the deaths of Margaret Appleby and Seth Windom."

If he was surprised by the request, he didn't show it. But maybe that was because Hulk was leaning on him with the bulk of her weight and digging her elbows into his muscles.

"Specifically," I continued, sitting on the edge of a plush leather recliner situated in a cluster of palm trees, "I'd like to ask you about your relationships with Margaret and Bertha Braun."

"*Un momentico, mi corazón.*" He pressed a button at the head of the massage table. "Minka, bring the *señorita un batido de mango y melón, por favor.*"

"Oon bahteedoe?" I asked.

He motioned toward a frozen drink garnished with a strawberry on a tray beside him. "A smoothie."

I sunk deeper into the chair and searched for the lever to the footrest. While I was here, I was going to make myself as comfortable as possible.

"You were saying, *cariño*?"

"Huh?" I looked up. "Oh, yeah. How did you know Margaret?"

"*Mi Margarita.*" He gave a deep sigh. "I met her a few years ago. She was the apple of my eye until I met *Berta*," he said, omitting the *h*.

"You know, Bertha came to my salon the day that Margaret was murdered."

"*Sí*," he confirmed, laying down and closing his eyes. "I saw her on the street outside, showing her makeup to two women."

Probably Eve and Loretta, I thought.

"Her eyes looked so mysterious, I could not resist her."

"Mysterious" is one word for it. "Monstrous" is another.

"I picked her up and took her straight to my bed."

"Wait," I said, both to stop him from adding any lurid details and to gather my thoughts. "You picked her up from The Clip and Sip? But I thought that she was going home to get ready for your dinner reservation."

"As we say in Cuba, '*El sexo es libre y el ron es barato*,' which means, 'Sex is free, and rum is cheap.' There is no need to spend money at an expensive restaurant when you have a beautiful woman on which to dine, no?"

I was so surprised that Bertha had an alibi that I didn't remember to be grossed out by his comment. But I did remember not to answer his rhetorical question.

Hulk cleared her throat. "It's time to turn over, Santiago."

He rolled over while she manipulated the linen. As he settled onto his back, he ogled her chichis. "*¡Ay, qué melones!*"

This time even I understood that the melons he was talking about weren't in a smoothie.

Hulk giggled and began stroking Santiago's legs with long, sweeping movements.

I shifted uncomfortably in my comfortable chair. "What about the night of the fundraiser for the lighthouse when Dr. Windom was killed? I saw Bertha talking to him at the Smugglers' Tavern, but I didn't see you."

"I wasn't feeling well," he replied with his eyes closed. "In fact, I began to have some pains in my chest. So I called her at the tavern to ask her advice, and she came here to drive me to the hospital."

"What time was that?"

"Six o'clock."

I leaned forward. "But that was around the time I saw her talking to Dr. Windom on the deck."

"*Sí, mi amor*. I am afraid that I interrupted their conversation."

"Okay, but what time did she drive you to the hospital?"

"At six thirty. And, according to the police, Dr. Windom died between seven thirty and nine thirty that night. At that time, Berta and I were in the emergency room." He turned to look at me and winked. "Getting frisky. So you see..." His voice trailed off as he opened his arms wide.

Minka floated into the room, handed me the *batido*, and left without a sound.

I hoped that there was some "ron" in the smoothie, because I needed a drink. I took a sip and marveled at the fact that Bertha had alibis for both of the murders. Now I knew why the police had released her, but I still had a few more questions I needed to ask. "Do you know whether Bertha ever lived in another state?"

"She told me that she has lived in this area her entire life."

I chewed on my smoothie straw for a moment and then decided to ask a dangerous question. "Did she ever mention the name Hazel Kirkpatrick?"

Santiago propped himself up, and his eyes had a strange glow. "Who is this Hazel?"

I wasn't sure how much he knew, if anything, so I had to be careful not to give too much away. "A woman in Jackson, Mississippi."

"Ah." His face fell. "She sounds like a *habanero*, the spicy pepper named after *La Habana*."

Now I understood the reason for that glow. I gulped down some smoothie and stood up. "Thank you for your time, Mr., I mean, Santiago."

"You're leaving so soon?" he asked as he moved to get off the table.

"Stay down!" I shouted as though I were talking to a dog, which, in a sense, was true.

"You can't stay for a while?" His eyes narrowed into a seductive stare. "I'll teach you to salsa Cuban style."

I wasn't sure what all that involved, but I was pretty sure that it wasn't just dancing. "Sorry, but I have an urgent errand to run." I held out my hands in a stay-put gesture. "I'll see myself out."

I turned and catapulted myself into the hallway and hotfooted it to the exit—in case Santiago was in the mood for a chase.

When I was safely locked inside the Ferrari in the resort parking lot, I wondered whether I'd been barking up the wrong palm tree where Bulldog was concerned. I hoped that I was, because Santiago would undoubtedly tell her about my visit. But on the other hand, I knew that an alibi didn't necessarily translate to innocence. After all, Amy could have been right about that drifter Clyde Willard being the brawn behind Bertha's brain.

As I pulled out of the parking lot, I turned in the direction of the library. I could think of only two more ways to rule Bertha out as a suspect, and for Lucy's sake, I was going to see to both of them before going to the police. Even if I had to die trying.

* * *

Amy held the scan gun to a book entitled *Funeral Flowers for Beginners* but then stopped dead in mid-scan. "Santiago Beltrán was buck naked?"

"Shh!" I waved my arms like the snakes in Medusa's hair. "The patrons can hear you."

She had a gleam in her eye not unlike that of Santiago's when he'd asked about Hazel. "Did you get a look at his *schwanz*?" She moved in close. "That's German for 'tail,'" she said out of one side of her mouth, "but it's also slang for 'penis.'"

"I'd kind of figured that," I said, glancing around to make sure that no one was within earshot. When this investigation was over, my next assignment would be to help Amy find a boyfriend. And from all indications, that was going to take some serious sleuthing skills.

She swiped the scanner and frowned. "The system can't read the barcode."

"Probably because the computer doesn't want the book returned." I wrinkled my mouth. "Who would want to read about funeral flowers anyway?"

"Viola Aster, the vice president of the Garden Club," she replied, entering the barcode number by hand. "Since Margaret has no known relatives, Viola has taken it upon herself to choose the flowers for her funeral, whenever that is, and George Fontaine down at Some Enchanted Florist has offered to cover the cost."

"That's nice of them." I leaned onto the counter. "What did Viola pick?"

"Blue forget-me-nots."

I looked at Amy like she'd just coldcocked me with the scan gun. "Is that supposed to be some kind of joke?"

She shrugged and placed the book on a cart. "You have to admit that it's a pretty good way to remember her."

"Okay, fine." Let's face it—the flower was spot on. "But Danger Cove is going to want to forget all about Margaret when the news breaks about her involvement in black-market adoptions."

I heard a gasp from behind me and turned to see a woman giving me a shame-on-you stare as she led a little girl away from the desk.

"Would you use your library voice, please?" Amy hissed.

It took everything I had not to call her the proverbial pot calling the kettle black.

"Did you finish going through the *Clarion-Ledger* microfiche?" I asked in an irritated whisper.

She nodded. "But I couldn't find anything to indicate that other families had pressed suit against the hospital."

I put my bag on the counter. It was getting heavy, like this conversation. "So, you're telling me that the Bible could be the only proof that more babies were stolen?"

"Unless there were other cases that were settled privately," she replied as she scanned another book.

I rubbed my forehead. The thought that twenty-nine mothers might still believe that their children had died was already overwhelming. The knowledge that I might have lost the only evidence to prove otherwise was almost too much to bear. "I just wish that I'd turned that Bible over to the police."

"Right?" Amy agreed in her typical show-no-mercy fashion. "But at least you can tell them who stole it."

"It's just my word against Clyde's at this point. What I can't figure out is how he knew what Margaret was up to, especially if Hazel Kirkpatrick was the only one of all those women who figured out that her baby had survived."

She pushed up her glasses. "He could have been an acquaintance or a relative who stumbled on the truth somehow."

"Hey, that would make sense," I said, pointing at her. "I'll bet that Clyde was blackmailing her, and then she threatened to report him, so he killed her." I pressed my finger to my cheek. "But wait. Then why kill Dr. Windom?"

"He must have been involved with the adoptions in some way. He was a doctor, after all."

"I suppose, but he didn't show up in any of the information on the case."

My ringtone sounded, and Amy gave me a librarian look.

"Sorry." I pulled my phone from my bag and glanced at the display. "It's Gia. I need to take this."

I hurried out the main door and pressed Accept. "Hi."

"So let me guess," Gia began. "You wrapped up your investigation but stayed at the resort to play a rousing game of beach-blanket bingo with the retirees."

She had no idea how close that was to being true, especially the rousing part. "Actually, I'm at the library doing some research. Is the plumber still there?"

"Yeah, it was supposed to be an easy job, but he's run into a problem."

"There goes more money I don't have down the drain," I said as I took a seat on a bench by the front door. "What's wrong now?"

"He removed two corroded pipes, but he can't put the new ones in because there's some kind of obstruction in the wall. He's got to go underneath the house to see if he can figure it out."

I saw four dollar signs on my mental cash register. "Well, I guess it's too late for a second bid. Who did Detective Ohlsen send to oversee him?"

"Some guy I don't know." She paused. "But I'd like to know him better."

The last thing I needed was Gia flirting with the policeman while the plumber was trying to work, although, come to think of it, her Medusa getup might actually make him finish the repairs faster. "Okay, but remember that I'm paying the plumber by the hour, so please let the men do their jobs."

"Just what are you implying?" she huffed. "You know that I'll wait until the leak is fixed to put the moves on the cop."

I rolled my eyes.

"By the way, right after you left this morning, Zac stopped by on his way to work to check on us. Isn't that adorable?"

My breath caught in my chest, and it wasn't because of Zac's sweet gesture. Clyde had just exited the hardware store across the street.

"I'll call you later." I jumped behind a shrub and shoved the phone into my bag.

I peered through the branches and watched as Clyde loaded boards into the back of a Pirate's Hook Marine Services truck. He was wearing a short-sleeved shirt that exposed the purplish-brown marks on his arms. The spots still seemed fairly pronounced, considering that the accident at the Marine had happened days before.

Clyde threw the last of the boards into the bed and then hopped into the truck and sped away.

As soon as the coast was clear, I went inside and found Amy shelving books in the stacks. "I just saw Clyde."

Her eyes grew wide behind her lenses, and she stepped behind the cart. "He's not coming in here, is he?"

"He's gone," I said, waving my hand to calm her. "Listen, can you think of an illness that causes dark-purple marks on the skin, like on the arms?"

"Well, my *Großvater* Spannagel had those from diabetes."

"Oh my gosh." I put my hand over my mouth. "Diabetes!"

"I appreciate your concern for my grandfather, Cass," she said, resuming her shelving. "But the old man's dead as a doornail."

I shook my head. Amy never failed to amaze me. "What I meant was that a lot of diabetics need regular insulin injections. If Clyde is one of them, then he probably has syringes with him at all times."

"If you're thinking that he injected Margaret with one of those syringes, think again. Like I told you, it takes at least fifty milliliters of Barbicide to kill someone, and insulin syringes hold a fraction of that amount, one milliliter maximum. So, he would have had to inject her at least fifty times—"

"Enough with the graphic details," I interrupted, holding out my hand in a stopping motion. "But he would've had easy access to syringes, right?"

"Everyone does. I order them online for crafting, especially when I'm gluing small items like rhinestones."

I sat down at one of the public computers. "Darn it. I was sure that I had him."

She inserted a book on a shelf. "What are you going to do now?"

I tapped the keyboard to wake the computer. "Try to find Hazel Kirkpatrick."

"What will you say to her if you do?" she asked, walking up behind me.

"I don't know yet," I replied as I googled whitepages.com. When the page loaded, I entered *Hazel Kirkpatrick* and *Jackson, MS*, and then hit the Return key.

There was a match.

I didn't need to look at Amy to know that she was as surprised as I was, because I could see her open-mouthed expression reflected on the screen.

I inhaled and pressed the link to Hazel's address. Her contact information appeared, and I glanced at the clock on the screen. It was ten thirty, so it wasn't too early to call. With shaking hands, I entered the number into my phone and pressed speaker so that Amy could listen.

"Hello?" a raucous female voice answered. She sounded annoyed.

"Hi, my name's Ca—uh, Cathy, and I'm calling for Hazel Kirkpatrick?" I said it as a question, not quite believing that I had the right person.

"You got me," she snapped. "But I divorced Mr. Kirkpatrick years ago, the no-good, lousy bum."

"I...I see," I faltered, unsure of what to say after her rant.

"The name's Hazel Wil—"

The connection cut out, and Amy laid a wallop on my back that sent the phone flying.

I fell to my knees as I scrambled to retrieve it, thinking that surely Hazel had been about to say "Williams" or "Wilkins" or something. When I reached the phone, I asked, "Could you please repeat that name, ma'am?"

"I said," she began, dragging the word into two syllables, "Willard."

And there it was—something that I should have suspected all along. Clyde was neither an acquaintance of nor a relation to Margaret Appleby. He was connected to Hazel.

CHAPTER FOURTEEN

Swallowing my stupor, I pressed forward with my investigation. "By any chance, Ms. Willard, do you know someone named Clyde?"

"Clyde?" she bellowed. "What the heck's he done now?"

I paused, caught off guard by her reply. Clyde had done a lot, but I could hardly tell her that.

"Who'd you say you were again?" she demanded. "You're not with the police, are you?"

"Uh, no, ma'am. I—"

I heard the sound of the receiver crashing down. Clearly, Ms. Willard didn't have a smartphone.

Amy gave me a shove. "Call her back."

"You heard how suspicious she was. She's not going to talk to me again."

She twisted her mouth to one side, as though debating whether to say something she shouldn't. "Do you think she's going to call Clyde?"

"Don't *you*?" I smacked my forehead with the palm of my hand. "Why did I have to say that my name was Cathy? Why not Brittany or Megan? Now Clyde will probably know it was me."

"Don't worry about that," she said in an unusually reassuring tone. "Think of it this way—he already knows you're onto him, so that phone call isn't going to make any difference."

My lips flattened. "How comforting."

She put her hand on her hips. "He's bound to be onto you by now, Cass. It's time to face the facts."

"Good point." I tapped my lips with my index finger. "But what are the facts? I mean, Clyde is onto me, but I still don't know who he is in all of this. Is he the stepfather or step-uncle of the child? Or, if Willard is Hazel's maiden name, is he a maternal uncle?"

"There's no way to know based on what Hazel said."

My phone vibrated in my hand, and I dropped it like a hot potato, thinking that it was Hazel. But when I looked down, I saw Gia's name on the display. "Let me guess," I said, mimicking her earlier greeting. "The plumber found hidden treasure in the wall, and now we're rich!"

"Come home now," Gia said without a trace of humor in her voice. "Do not pass Go. Do not collect $200."

The line went dead.

Amy resumed her shelving. "That was fast."

"Yeah, short and not at all sweet," I said. Because if I had interpreted Gia's Monopoly-speak correctly, I was going directly to jail.

* * *

I stood in the middle of The Clip and Sip, wondering what was going on. This certainly wasn't the homecoming I'd expected. There were no squad cars out front, no officers waiting to read me my rights, not even a warrant for my arrest. It wasn't like I was disappointed—quite the contrary. But the fear I'd felt for myself was turning into concern for Gia. What if she'd called me because she was the one in trouble?

And then I thought about Clyde.

"Gia?" I shouted.

There was no reply.

"Is anyone here?"

The building was silent.

My pulse started to quicken, but I reminded myself that I'd seen the plumber's truck and the officer's unmarked car parked on the street as I'd pulled the Ferrari around back. Then it occurred to me that the officer might be with the plumber underneath the building.

I hurried to the stairwell and pulled out my phone. With every step I took, my worry intensified. "Gia?" I called with my finger hovering above 9-1-1 in my contact list. "If you're here, please answer me."

"Upstairs," she replied in a muffled tone.

I stopped near the landing, grabbed the railing, and bowed my head. I didn't know why Gia had sounded stifled, but it had better be because she was bound and gagged. Otherwise, I was going to tie her up myself.

When I finally found her, I knew why she hadn't heard me. For one thing, she was inside Vinnie's old bathroom. And for another, she was mesmerized by the Rambo-sized ribcage of the twenty-something-year-old officer, who, in turn, was bewitched by her Chicken Filleted chest.

"Sorry to interrupt," I said from the doorway. "But what's going on here?"

"I've almost got it," a gruff voice announced from below.

I stepped inside the bathroom to find the plumber on his hands and knees with his torso inside the antique vanity that contained the sink. Then I stepped right back outside. There was an enormous crack down there, and it wasn't in the floor. "Almost got what?"

Gia tore her eyes from the officer's buff bod. "He found a box in the wall, and he's trying to get it out."

The officer sprung into action—and so did his Dolce & Gabbana cologne. "The box was originally located to the right of the trap door under the sink, Miss Conti. But when Jim here removed the old pipes, it fell into the space where the pipes had been."

I gave him the once-over. "And you are?"

He flashed a smooth smile and lowered his already low brow. "Officer Stallone at your service."

Stallone? Suddenly, everything became clear to me. "Gia, can I talk to you alone for a minute?"

She leapt to her feet and jerked me by the elbow into the hallway. "I thought you'd never ask. Isn't he *friggin' fab*? His name is Donatello, which is perfect, because he's totally a Greek god."

His name was perfect all right. "Donatello was the Renaissance painter that inspired the Teenage Mutant Ninja Turtle. I think you mean Dionysus."

"Donatello, Dionysus." She made a dismissive gesture. "Whatever."

My sentiments exactly. "So, would you mind explaining why you made me rush home like that? You scared me half to death."

She gave a so-what shrug. "Donatello said that the homeowner had to give consent to open the box."

That did it. After the plumber and the Greek god of the Ninja Turtles left, I was going to hog-tie her Texas style.

"Don't you get it? This could be it." Gia squealed and rubbed her hands together. "Vinnie's missing money."

Although I was skeptical, I had to admit that I was a little excited. After all, what else would Vinnie hide inside a wall if not some ill-gotten gains?

Officer Stallone entered the hallway. "With your permission, ma'am, I'd like to have the plumber open the box, given the ongoing investigations associated with your property."

"Of course," I said.

We followed Officer Stallone to the bathroom, and he raised a manicured thumb at the plumber. "Yo, you're good to go, bro."

Jim nodded and pulled a hammer from his tool belt. Then he stuck his tongue out to one side and began prying the lid from the crude wooden box.

I was so nervous that I thought I was going to pass out from the anticipation—or from Officer Stallone's cologne.

"Got it," Jim grunted when he removed the last nail. As he lifted the lid, I squeezed my eyes shut and said a silent prayer—for cold, hard cash.

"Leaping lasagna," Gia exclaimed. "It's blue."

Blue? Didn't she mean green? I opened my eyes and looked down at the box. It was filled with hundreds, maybe thousands, of light-blue, diamond-shaped pills encased in clear plastic sheets.

Jim rose to his feet and pulled up his pants. He exchanged an uneasy look with the officer. "I'd best get back to those, uh, pipes."

I turned to Officer Stallone. "What is this stuff?"

"I'm afraid that it's Viagra, ma'am." He shot Gia a penetrating look. "But I don't know that from personal experience or nuttin', yo."

So Uncle Vinnie *was* dealing drugs, although certainly not the kind I'd expected, and they were blue.

Gia gasped. "So, that's how Vinnie did it."

"Did what?" I asked.

"You know, *it*." She gave me a nudge. "As in, hiding the cannoli, bringing the al dente noodle to the spaghetti house—"

"Okay, okay," I interrupted. "You've made it unappetizingly clear."

"The Don Juan of Danger Cove was taking vats of Viagra." She flailed her arms into a *V* to reiterate her point.

Officer Stallone clutched his six-pack abs and laughed like a high school football player at a nerd convention. "Yo, everyone in town knew that old Vinnie got a lotta action and all, but if the dude needed this much blue diamond…"

I cocked my head to the side. "What did you say?"

"Pardon me, ma'am," he said, resuming his police persona. "I shouldn't have disparaged your relation in your presence."

"Not that," I said, exasperated. "The last thing you said—blue diamond."

"That's a street name for Viagra, and I shouldn't have used such a crude phrase in your company."

I didn't have time to be annoyed by his brownnosing, because another piece of the puzzle had just slipped into place.

"We used to have a problem with the illegal sale of Viagra here in Danger Cove, especially down at the Coveside Retirement Resort. Those old geezers were popping them like they were blue Skittles or something, and EMS was having to go out there every week because of all the side effects. Did you know that if you take enough of that stuff, you could start seeing blue?"

I didn't, but I could definitely relate.

"Then about a year or so ago," he continued, "the Viagra disappeared, just like that." He looked down at the box and raised his Neanderthal brow as though a light bulb had just turned on in his in head.

Gia and I exchanged a concerned look.

"So yo," Officer Stallone began with a combined hip-and-arm thrust more reminiscent of Elvis than Sylvester, "you ladies know that I'm going to have to report this discovery to Detective Ohlsen, right?"

Gia batted gold-flecked eyelashes at the officer. "Donatello, could you give us a moment?"

Hooking his thumbs into his duty belt, he continued the unintentional Elvis impersonation by jutting out his pelvis and curling his lip at Gia. "Don't keep me waitin' too long, *awright*?"

She giggled and twisted a curl around her finger.

This time I jerked her by the elbow to my bedroom. "Forget the flirting, cuz. We've got big problems."

"I know," she said, closing the door. "*Bobby Darin* and *bd* are codes for *blue diamond.*"

"Which Uncle Vinnie was dealing to Danger Cove," I added.

She collapsed on the edge of my bed. "What should we do?"

"Turn his little black book over to the police," I replied. Then a terrible thought struck me. "Wait. We still have it, don't we? Or did Clyde steal that too?"

"Relax. It's in my room with the copy I made." She flipped her hair. "But seriously, can we afford yet another scandal in the family?"

"What choice do we have? Officer Stallone has already seen the Viagra."

Gia stuck out her silicone. "I can take care of that, *cug*."

"We may live in an old brothel," I said, "but I'm not about to pimp you out to the police."

"It's not like I mind." She licked her lips. "Donatello's my dream date."

I refrained from comment—it would've been like shooting turtles in a barrel. "I'm not saying that you can't go out with him. I just don't think that your date should involve bribing him to hide evidence from the police."

"I don't get you sometimes." She flopped backward on my bed. "You say that you want to save your business and your reputation, but then you want to do something like this."

"Let me put it into perspective for you. Two people are dead from Barbicide poisoning, one of whom died in this very salon. And now blue pills turn up in our house, the place where Vinnie died."

She propped herself on her elbows. "Are you saying there's a connection?"

"I'm not sure. But Clyde is related to one of the babies in Margaret's Bible, so anything is possible."

Gia sat up and grabbed my forearm. "So, he *is* the one who snuck into our salon and killed her!"

"It makes sense. He supposedly peeps into windows. Maybe he looked inside The Clip and Sip, saw Margaret, and seized his opportunity."

"But why kill her now? He's not new to town, is he?"

"I don't think so, but I can find out." I put my hands on my hips. "The point, though, is that it's getting too complicated and too dangerous for us to investigate these murders."

"You know something?" she asked, her eyes full of wonder. "I actually agree with you."

"That's almost as alarming as your Medusa look," I replied, only half joking.

She stood up and socked me in the arm. "I'll go get Vinnie's book."

As soon as she left, I sat at my desk and wrote a list of my findings for Detective Ohlsen. I included the Bible, Margaret's true identity, Hazel Kirkpatrick, a.k.a. Willard, and, of course, Clyde.

"Here it is." Gia stood in the doorway with the black book in her hand.

"Awesome," I said, tucking the note into an envelope. "Give it to Officer Stallone, and have him deliver this letter to Detective Ohlsen."

She took the envelope from my hand. "What is it?"

"A list of all the evidence I've collected."

Her eyes narrowed to slits. "Why can't you give it to him?" she asked, and then her eyes popped. "You're not leaving town, are you?"

I shook my head. "I'm not going to cut and run this time. I ran out on school, my ex, Texas, and even Zac the other day. If

I want to save the salon and my future, I have to stand my ground for once and fight."

"I'm proud of you, Cass," she said, raising her fist and bumping it against mine. "But how do you plan to do that if you're ratting yourself out to Detective Ohlsen?"

"I'm going to the Pirate's Hook Marine Services to talk to Zac about Clyde."

Her head snapped back. "What? You just said that we were in over our heads with this investigation. Why don't you just let the police handle Clyde from here?"

"I am, which is why I wrote that note to Detective Ohlsen. But remember," I began, pointing at my chest, "I'm the one who lost the evidence."

"So?"

"So, I have to do this. For Lucy, for us." I paused and stared out the window. "And for twenty-nine of those babies in that Bible."

* * *

I peered around the bow of the sailboat and stared at the service entrance to the Pirate's Hook Marine Services. I'd been camped out in the dry dock area since twelve thirty waiting for a chance to talk to Zac without Clyde seeing me. A half an hour had now passed, and Zac still hadn't replied to my voice message or text asking him to come outside. I was starting to think that he was ignoring me.

My "Cut Your Hair" ringtone blasted from the pocket of my DKNY yellow trench coat. I pulled out my phone in a panic and pressed mute. The caller was none other than Detective Ohlsen. By now he'd probably read the contents of my note and sent a squad car after me. Or maybe he was coming to arrest me himself. Either way, his call was my cue to make a move while I still had the freedom to do so.

I shoved the phone back into my pocket, put on my hood, and headed for the Marine. When I walked around to the front of the building, I almost fainted. The company truck was parked near the main door, and the lumber that Clyde had purchased from the hardware store was still in the back. Fortunately for me, he wasn't behind the wheel.

Lowering my head, I opened the door and entered the showroom.

The sixty-something man behind the counter arranged his comb-over with thick fingers. "May I help you, miss?"

"Yes," I replied in a soft voice. "Is Zac Taylor available?"

He pointed toward the cove. "He's out on the dock prepping a boat for a potential buyer."

"Thanks." I turned and hurried outside. The wind was picking up, so I pulled my hood tight.

I scanned the Marine's private dock and spotted Zac unfurling a sail. As I walked toward the boat, I kept one eye out for Clyde and the other fixed on Zac. He looked so sure of himself as he stood on the stern and hauled the line to raise the mainsail. And so strong. My eyes—okay, both of them—drifted to his biceps. Then I shook my head. I'd been hanging out with Gia and Amy for too long.

When I arrived at the boat, I wondered whether Zac had heard me approaching over the sound of the flags flapping and the metal cables clinking against the sailboat masts. If he had, he gave no indication of it. "Hi, Zac."

He looked over at me and then began cleating off the rope. "Hey."

I was definitely getting the cold shoulder. "Gia said that you came by the house this morning to check on us. Thank you for doing that."

"You're welcome." He walked to the jib and began hauling the line.

I glanced at the cabin. "Is Clyde with you?"

He stopped hoisting for a moment and then resumed. "I haven't seen him for an hour or so. He's probably at lunch." He fell silent. "Is this about the investigation?"

There was no point in lying to Zac any longer. He already knew about Clyde, and right now I needed him on my side. "Yes. Do you mind if I come aboard?"

"Be my guest," he replied, his eyes still focused on the sail.

I leapt onto the bow and stepped into the cockpit.

Zac secured the rope and wiped his brow. "After everything that's happened, why wouldn't you just leave it to the police?"

I took a deep breath. "Because I feel responsible for the Bible that he stole from my house. It contains information that affects countless individuals, so, if possible, I'd like to find it before he destroys it or uses it to hurt anyone."

"And how are you planning to do that, exactly?" he exclaimed. "By searching his house?"

I could see that he was angry, and I didn't blame him. After all, I'd deliberately misled him about my interest in Clyde. I took a seat and replied, "That's what I wanted to talk to you about."

"No way, Cassidi," he said, wagging his index finger. "Even if I knew his address, I wouldn't give it to you." He tugged at the collar of his windbreaker as though letting off steam. "If Clyde is guilty of the murders, which is doubtful, then the last thing you need to do is go and break into his house."

Now it was my turn to get a little hot under my hood. Who was Zac Taylor to doubt me and tell me what I did or didn't need to do? "Why are you so sure he's innocent?"

He put his hands on his hips and hovered over the seating area. "Because, unlike you, I believe that everyone is innocent until proven guilty." He released his arms and turned to face the ocean. "And besides, Clyde's been in Danger Cove for only six months or so. What motive could he possibly have had to murder two people?"

So Clyde *was* new to town. I wasn't going to say anything, but my temper got the best of me. "What if I told you that he was either the stepfather or the uncle of a baby that Margaret stole and then sold on the black market in the early '80s?"

Zac blinked, shocked by this news, but he quickly regained his composure. "Then I'd tell you that you were dead wrong about the guy. Because I happen to know that he was born on the same day as one of my sisters in 1981."

I was so surprised that I leapt to my feet. "How is that even possible? He looks like he's in his fifties."

"That's what diabetes and hard living will do to you."

"Why didn't you tell me all of this when I asked you about him at The Apple Tree?"

He pointed a finger at me. "Because you said that you wanted to hire him, and I didn't think that his health and his age were relevant."

He had me there.

"Little did I know that you were using me to spy on Clyde," he continued as he stepped into the cockpit to face me.

He was standing so close that I could feel the heat from his body through my trench coat, which was making it impossible for me to focus on staying mad. "Zac, it's not that I wanted to use you. I just didn't want to involve you in this whole mess and cause problems between you and your workmate."

"Well, you could've fooled me." He lifted the seat perpendicular to mine and removed a bucket. "Oh, and guess what? You did." He slammed the seat shut. "Now if you don't mind, I have to sponge off the deck before a client comes."

I didn't need to be asked to leave twice. I exited the boat and then turned to look at him. "For what it's worth, I'm on my way to the police station to tell Detective Ohlsen everything I know."

He began filling the bucket with water.

Clearly, this conversation was over.

I walked up the dock with a heavy heart. Zac was no longer speaking to me, and I was on my way to jail to serve time. On top of that, I was 99.9 percent sure that Clyde was one of the thirty babies that Margaret, a.k.a. Leona, had sold on the black market. And to be honest, I felt sorry for him in a way because I suspected that the trauma of the being taken from his birth mother had a lasting impact that might have even contributed to his criminal activity.

A wave hit the dock, bringing me crashing back to reality. I glanced at the sky and saw ominous-looking clouds gathering like vultures moving in for the kill. Judging from the size of the waves coming in, the storm was going to be a memorable one.

I tightened the belt of my trench and turned right toward Main Street. As I passed by the public dock, I looked at the slip where Prudence had docked her boat and was surprised to see that it was still there. In dire need of a friendly face, I decided to pay her a farewell visit.

As I neared the boat, Prudence emerged from the cabin clutching her left wrist. Then with one hand she began removing the canvas cover from the mainsail.

"Do you need any help with that?" I called.

She looked up and gave an embarrassed grin. "I've got it. Can you believe that I sprained my wrist opening a jar of mayonnaise?"

"Those lids can be murder," I replied as I reached the bow. "So, today's the big day, huh?"

She nodded as she unfastened the twist-locks holding the cover in place. "I've done everything I wanted to do here, so it's time to move on."

I eyed the darkening sky. "What about the storm?"

"According to the weather reports, I have just enough time to make it out of the area before the rain hits." The corners of her mouth turned up into a smirk-smile. "Besides, it's more fun to sail in choppy water."

"Well, you'll never know how much I envy you." For a split second, I thought about begging her to take me with her. I mean, who wouldn't be tempted to give up an old whorehouse and a sinking salon in exchange for her freedom? But then I remembered my earlier vow to Gia to stand my ground and fight for my future. *Darn it.*

Prudence turned the last twist-lock, and a gust of wind blew the cover from the mast. It landed draped over the bow, hanging partially in the water.

I crouched and pulled the cover onto the dock, revealing the boat registration information on the side of the bow. I'd gone sailing with friends in Texas often enough to know that the state abbreviation came before the actual registration number. But instead of seeing the *CA* abbreviation for Prudence's home state of California, I saw *MS*. And even though I had a mental block when it came to the abbreviations for Missouri and Mississippi, this time I had no doubt about what that *MS* stood for.

I looked up at Prudence in a state of shock, and her face hardened.

Our eyes locked.

With her good hand, she drew a gun from the back of her waistband and cocked the hammer. "As we say down South," she drawled, "'keep your saddle oiled and your gun greased.'"

I started to inform her that the saying was specifically Texan, but then I concluded that under the circumstances it might be best to keep my mouth shut.

She leveled the gun between my eyes, and as I stared down the barrel, jail started looking pretty good.

"Stand up, and step onto the boat," she said in an even tone.

Fear began washing over me like the waves on the dock, but somehow my body obeyed her order.

"Now get into the cabin."

As I opened the hatch and descended the stairs, it struck me that I was going to be sailing away with Prudence after all.

At least, I hoped that was the plan.

CHAPTER FIFTEEN

When I reached the bottom of the cabin steps, I came to an abrupt stop.

Clyde was on a couch to my right, staring at me with the intensity of a lion preparing to pounce on its prey.

"I don't have all day," Prudence said through clenched teeth. "Move it." She pushed me between my shoulder blades.

I hit the kitchen cabinet directly in front of me so hard that my upper body slammed onto the countertop. I planted my feet on the ground and raised my head to find out whether Clyde was coming for me next.

"Stay down," she ordered. "And put your hands behind your back."

I complied.

As she began to bind my wrists with thick plastic cords, I saw that Clyde's arms were in an unnatural position behind his back and that his feet were tied together with what appeared to be plastic airline handcuffs.

Now I knew how Prudence had really hurt her wrist, but nothing else about the situation made sense. A million questions were running through my mind, but I limited myself to the most pressing one. "What are you going to do to us?"

She finished tying my hands and knelt to bind my ankles. "To put it in the language of our people, you and Clyde are going to sleep with the fishes."

I wasn't sure what she meant by that "our people" comment, but if she was implying that I was a wannabe *mafiosa*, then she had me all wrong. "I think you're confusing me with Gia."

The boat lurched, and I hit the counter once again. It served me right for that cousin crack.

Prudence opened the curtain on the window above the kitchen sink. "The storm's picking up. I've got to get this boat into open water."

"Maybe we shouldn't go," I gushed. "I know you don't care about us, but you could be swept off the boat in weather like this."

She closed the curtain. "I'll take that over staying here and getting arrested. Now, Chatty *Cathy*," she began with a telltale stare, "you sit across from Clyde." Her fingers sunk into the flesh of my arm as she yanked me upright and threw me onto the other couch. "I'm sure you two have a lot to talk about since he says you're friends with his mother, and all."

I squirmed to a sitting position as Prudence rushed from the cabin. So, Hazel had called Clyde, and he'd put two and two together and reported it to Prudence. But what reason did Prudence have to want to kill him? And who was she in all of this anyway?

The outboard engine roared to life, and the sailboat jerked as it pulled away from the dock.

While Prudence motored us out to sea, I pondered an escape plan. My phone was still in the pocket of my coat, but there was no hope of reaching it with my hands tied. I leaned my head against the wall as I realized with a sinking feeling—the *I'm about to plunge to the bottom of the Pacific Ocean* variety—that the only way I had a shot at freedom was to convince Prudence to cut me loose. Then I started my breathing exercises.

Clyde started hacking like a two-pack-per-day smoker.

I studied his leather skin and wispy hair, amazed that he was only in his thirties. And then I remembered something—Prudence had said that she was a decade older than I was, which would make her around the same age as Clyde. My mind flashed to that page in Margaret's Bible, and suddenly I knew who she was. "Prudence is one of the other babies that Margaret and the crooked obstetrician she worked with, Jonas Thorpe, sold on the black market. Just like you."

He showed no reaction. "Nosy till the end, ain't ya?"

"I'm trying to find out the truth."

He cough-laughed. "What for?" He glanced around the cabin for emphasis. "Whaddaya think you're gonna do with that information here?"

The motor shut off, and the boat started swaying.

I broke into a cold sweat. We'd reached the bay, and we were about to set sail to our final resting places.

Despite this grim realization, I knew that I had to do two things if I wanted to survive—stay positive and win Clyde over. He wasn't in the best health, but he was still stronger than I was. And I might need his strength to get out of this nightmare alive. "We could make it off this boat, you know."

He snorted and shook his head.

"And if we do," I continued, undaunted by his doubt, "I would think that you would feel some responsibility toward the other people who were stolen from their parents."

He shifted his hips. "Some of 'em probably figured it out when they grew up, like Prudence did."

There was the confirmation—Prudence was one of Margaret's victims. "But what about the ones who didn't?"

Clyde stared at me, expressionless.

I tried an emotional approach. "I'm sure that you suffered serious trauma after being taken from your mother, maybe enough to make you kill for revenge. So, don't you want to make things right for the other victims?"

The deep lines on his forehead relaxed. "I didn't kill nobody."

I should've been skeptical, but I was too surprised. It had never occurred to me that Prudence might have committed the murders, even after she'd pointed that gun in my face. "But I saw you in Margaret's house."

He gave me a hard stare. "I seen you there too, and you didn't kill nobody neither."

I paused, unsure what to think. Even if Clyde wasn't a killer, he was still a thief and a snake. "If you didn't kill anyone, then what were you doing searching through Margaret's things?"

"Workin'," he replied as though breaking and entering constituted an honest day's labor. "Prudence hired me to help her find evidence of the adoptions. She never said she was gonna murder no one."

"Why didn't you turn her in after Margaret was found dead? Or at least quit your, uh, job?"

"I figured I could get more money outta Prudence. And frankly, I didn't care that the old broad got killed. She had it comin'."

So that was why Prudence wanted to kill off Clyde. He was blackmailing her. "You also broke into my house to get the Bible and the syringe wrapper."

He nodded. "When I told Prudence I seen you at Leona's, she figured you'd found sumpthin' that connected Leona to the adoptions in that ottoman with the fake bottom. I thought she'd hidden a document or some type o' information in a book or a drawer, but neither of us knew what we was lookin' for till I found the Bible at your place. And you mentioning the syringe wrapper to Prudence was a lucky break. She didn't know where that thing had got off to, but she knew it had her fingerprints on it."

I mentally kicked myself for being such a *stunad*. "That explains why you didn't take the wrapper when you planted that prescription pad in my trash." I looked him in the eyes. "What I don't understand is why Dr. Windom had to die."

He met my gaze. "Because he's her ma's brother, and she found out that he was the one who helped her ma adopt her from Leona and Thorpe. So she offed him."

The stern of the boat rose and fell, causing both of us to slide down the couches. But that didn't shake me nearly as much as the shocking news about Dr. Windom.

I wiggled my way back to the corner of the couch and pressed my feet to the floor. "If Dr. Windom facilitated Prudence's adoption, he must have known Margaret."

"Nah." Clyde used his legs to push himself up. "He was friends with Doc Thorpe. Prudence said they went to med school together back in Jackson."

So Mississippi had been at the heart of this whole mess. "Then how did Margaret end up in the same town as Dr. Windom?"

A bitter smile flickered across his lips. "Because they was lovers. I guess at some point they split up."

Something cold touched my foot, and I looked down and saw an inch of water on the floor—a sure sign that we had a hole in the hull. I licked my lips and pressed on. "What happened to Jonas Thorpe?"

"Prudence tracked him down in New Mexico, livin' under an assumed name. She said he died of a stroke back in 2007."

The boat bounced as it struck wave after wave, and something inside one of the kitchen cabinets started knocking into the door.

"Did Prudence find out about this recently? Is that why she killed them now?"

He glanced at the water on the floor. "She's known she was adopted since she was in high school. She found some letter her uncle had written to her ma about it. But she only tracked me down about eight months ago when Windom stopped makin' payments."

"What kind of payments?"

"Prudence was blackmailing him. She told him that if he didn't pay up, she was gonna turn him in. Since most of his patients was on Medicare, he didn't make big bucks like other docs. So he started a drug ring to come up with the cash. But then his dealer quit, and he stopped payin'."

This was turning out to be one wild ride—the story and the sailboat.

"Then she was never a hospital administrator in LA," I said to myself.

"No, but she was in Jackson. She got a master's in hospital administration so she could work at Presley-Smith Memorial."

I cringed at this last detail. Prudence had been bent on revenge for years. Nothing was going to stop her now.

"She went there lookin' to find out who her real parents was, and that's how she found out she'd been declared dead as a baby," he continued. "She also got records of all the other babies who supposedly died in Thorpe's delivery room, which is why she needed that Bible—to figure out which ones died for real and which ones was sold."

I narrowed my eyes. "What did she want to do with that information?"

"She had this plan to track down the adoptive parents and make 'em pay for what they did. We was gonna blackmail 'em and split the money sixty/forty. That forty percent was supposed to be my 401(k)."

Before I could comment on Clyde's choice of retirement plans, the waves began tossing the boat about like it was a child's toy. We struggled along with the boat to stay upright.

The thumping sound in the kitchen had stopped, but now the cabinet door was slamming. Whatever was inside must have come out.

I glanced toward the kitchen and saw the Bible sliding down the walkway between the couches—in the inch of water. Fortunately, only the bottom of the book was submerged. But if the water continued to rise, the names of the other twenty-eight babies would be lost.

The hatch door flew open, and a soaking-wet Prudence appeared in the doorway.

I almost jumped out of my handcuffs at the sight of her. Except for the life jacket, she looked like Medusa incarnate.

She smirked and rubbed her wrist. "You know how to sail, right, Conti?"

I noticed that she'd switched to my last name—it was less personal that way. "I can work the jib pretty well."

"Good, because I need you on deck." She hurried down the steps and tripped over the Bible. "What the heck?"

I watched with relief as she grabbed the book and threw it in the sink. There was now a chance that the Bible would be saved. With any luck, I would be too.

She pulled out a pocketknife and cut my bindings. "Now get out there."

I exited the cabin first and grabbed onto the boat railing for dear life as I stepped into the cockpit.

Prudence took a seat in the rear and took hold of the tiller.

There was no point in asking for a life jacket, but I was determined to ask everything I wanted to know about the crimes, even though the stormy setting wasn't exactly conducive to conversation. Besides, growing up half Italian had taught me nothing if not how to talk loud. "I know why you killed Margaret, but why did you do it in my salon?"

She looked down as though debating whether to confess. "I didn't know she'd be there that day. So after you cut my hair, I came back to the boat and got one of the syringes I keep on hand to fix the fiberglass boat hull. Then I went back to The Clip and Sip and injected Margaret while she was asleep under the dryer."

I grimaced. "Did she put up a fight?"

"She never woke up. She was in a dead sleep."

That was one way to look at it. "Then you had Clyde set up Lucy."

She tightened her grip on the tiller. "You were the original target."

I gasped. "What? Why me?"

The boat hit a swell and dropped with a bang onto the water, but Prudence seemed too caught up in her memories to care.

"Thanks to the intervention of my dear Uncle Seth, Leona, a.k.a. Margaret, and Jonas Thorpe, I grew up the only child of a strict Southern Baptist couple who despised me." She paused. "But I was born to Italian American parents who already had four children."

That explained the Italian connection. "I'm sorry to hear that."

She gave an incredulous laugh. "Not as sorry as I am. I could've been a Francesca or a Bella in a big, happy family. But instead I ended up a Prudence in an abusive home."

The sail luffed, and she jerked the tiller.

I ducked just before the boom from the mainsail swung over my head to the other side of the boat. I scrambled to uncleat the jib and pull it in on the mainsail's side.

Clearly, I wasn't going to get a heads-up.

"Can you imagine being saddled with a name like Prudence?" she shouted over the wind. "The obvious root word is *prude*." She shook her head. "You're lucky you got Cassidi."

I could have pointed out that my name rhymed with "chastity" and that men routinely called me "Butch" or "David," but I made it a policy never to divulge that information to anyone. "Okay, but what does your adoption have to do with me?"

Her eyes hardened. "I could tell from your relationship with your cousin and from the fact that your uncle left you his salon that you had the big, happy Italian family I was supposed to have. And I was envious."

I started to tell her that with divorced parents and a murdered uncle, my family was hardly happy. But I didn't want to rock the boat—that is, not any more than the storm was already doing.

The wind shifted yet again, and we listed hard to the side.

I glanced nervously at the mainsail and then at Prudence. She was staring off in the distance, seemingly unaware of the danger. In part to placate her and in part because I meant it, I said, "I really wish that you'd gotten the childhood you deserved."

She blinked, and her bottom lip quivered. "I'm going to tack."

Relief washed over me—along with a wave. I stood up and pulled the rope to release it from its cleat, and then I knelt as the boom swung over my head to the opposite side of the boat. I wrapped the rope around the winch, pulled it tight, and cleated it.

"What I didn't count on was that hairdresser of yours having a past," she continued. "When the police brought her in for the second time, I had Clyde bury the syringes beneath her window. As long as someone took the fall, I didn't care who it was."

My temper flared at her indifference, but I was careful to keep it in check. I mean, she *was* a murderer, after all. "Why did you use Barbicide?"

She gave a half smile. "I got the idea while you were cutting my bangs. You pulled a comb from that jar of Barbicide on your station, and I realized how perfect it was."

"I don't understand. How was it perfect?"

"Margaret and Jonas told my birth parents that I died right after I was born—from blue baby syndrome."

The boat rolled, as did my stomach. *So that's why she turned them blue.*

Prudence doubled over, and I thought it was because of the storm. But when she straightened, she was wiping tears of laughter from her eyes. "The Barbicide was also funny because of the Viagra."

My head shot up. "What Viagra?"

"Didn't you figure that out?" she asked in a shrill voice. "Your uncle was running an illegal Viagra ring for my uncle."

I was so blown away by this bombshell that you could have knocked me over with a boom. "My Uncle Vinnie was Dr. Windom's drug dealer?"

"Actually, my uncle's ex-nurse, Bertha Braun, made the deliveries."

So, Bertha had been involved, albeit not in the way that I'd thought.

"They called her 'BD,' and she's the reason I'm here."

"Hold on." I wasn't sure I'd heard her correctly over the flapping of the sails. "Did you say 'BD?'"

"Yeah, for *Bulldog*."

It suddenly hit me. *BD* was code for the entire Viagra operation—blue diamond, a.k.a. Bobby Darin, and old Bulldog herself. "Are you saying that she's behind the murders?"

"Indirectly. About a year ago, my uncle announced that he couldn't pay me anymore because the insurance companies were taking a bigger cut of his profits. I paid him a surprise visit to find out what was really going on, and I discovered that he'd not only been helping Margaret make a nice little life for herself here in Danger Cove, but that he was also paying Bertha instead of me."

"Why was he doing that?" I asked, almost afraid to hear the answer.

"He had to fire her after she tried to kill one of his patients, so as to not raise the suspicion of the police. When she found herself without a job, she started blackmailing him. Apparently, his sister and brother-in-law weren't the only childless couple he'd referred to his old classmate, and as his longtime nurse, Bertha had made it her business to stay apprised of the details."

Now that I finally knew the whole sordid tale, I wasn't seeing blue anymore, not even in the middle of the ocean. All I could see was red. There had been so much greed and deceit and senseless killing that it pushed me over the edge—of reason, obviously.

I clenched my fists and stood up defiantly in the storm. "Did you kill my uncle?"

Prudence opened her mouth.

I waited for the words, but none came.

Instead, she screamed.

There was a tremendous crash, and I went sailing—unfortunately, not on the boat, but through the air. Then I plunged into the icy depths of the ocean like a cannonball shot from a pirate ship.

Once I recovered from the shock, I considered surrendering to the sea. I wasn't a strong enough swimmer to survive the storm, and I knew that as soon as I came up for air, Prudence would try to shoot me. Then I remembered what I'd said to Gia—I was going to stand my ground and fight. For her and for me, I had to make good on that vow. I just wished that I had some ground to stand on.

I started kicking and clawing with all my might. When I surfaced, Pirate's Hook was right in front of me—like a mirage. I swam toward it, but waves were breaking over my head, shoving me downward and force-feeding me mouthfuls of the frigid salt water.

This was not going swimmingly.

My anxiety was near panic attack level, and there was no way to do my 5-2-5 breathing in the middle of a turbulent ocean. Just when I thought that I'd be paying a visit to Davy Jones's locker, I remembered what Zac told me about the sea lions. I relaxed as best I could in an attempt to body surf, and the waves began washing me toward the rock. But when I arrived at the flat surface beneath the hook, my teeth were chattering, and my limbs were numb. There was no way I could make the climb up the slick side.

I floated further down the formation, desperate to find a way up. Finally, I got a foothold on some jutting rocks and pulled myself onto the platform. I collapsed on my stomach, shaking and gulping air in a daze.

Before I understood what was happening, an octopus wrapped itself around my neck and began to squeeze. I reached for the tentacles to free myself from its powerful grasp.

But they were fingers.

"You thought you were going to get away, didn't you?" Prudence snarled in my ear.

Terror flooded through me. I couldn't speak, because she was crushing my esophagus. I tried hitting her injured wrist, but she didn't let up.

She was too full of rage.

And I was suffocating.

Hot tears streamed down my cheeks. *Was this the end?*

As though in reply, a massive wave swept over the rock. It propelled me against the base of the hook where I clung for my life. But it lifted Prudence and thrust her into the point of the hook with such force that a piece of rock broke from the tip.

She washed out to sea.

Frantic, I scanned the area for Prudence. There was no sign of her in the water, so I looked up at the hook. A gleam of light caught my eye. I thought that I was seeing stars, but then I realized that there was only one. And it didn't sparkle—it glinted, like the sun peeking through the clouds. I wanted to reach out and grab that sun and pull its warmth to me. So I did. And I put it in my coat pocket.

Then the world went dark.

CHAPTER SIXTEEN

A fishtail was flapping against my face.

One of these days I was going to have a talk with that Filly Filipuzzi. I mean, it was one thing for his fish to take over my Dumpster, but it was entirely another for them to invade my house.

"Cassidi," a husky, male voice called. "Wake up."

I turned over, wanting to sleep a little longer. Then it registered that Zac was the one telling me to get up—and patting my cheek with his hand. But hang on. *Were we in bed together?* I'd pegged him as a smooth talker, but you'd think that I would've remembered him talking me into this.

Zac gently rolled me onto my back and cradled the back of my neck in his strong hand.

It was heaven. I felt so warm and protected.

His lips touched mine, and he…pinched my nose and started to blow?

My eyes fluttered open. The first thing I saw was Zac giving me mouth-to-mouth resuscitation, and then I noticed the point of Pirate's Hook looming over his head. The realization of where I was and what had happened came flooding back to me like a geyser.

I pushed Zac away and started coughing up water. After regurgitating a quart or two, I laid back on the jacket he'd placed beneath me. If there had been a chance of us getting together, I figured that my H2O heave-ho might've just put a damper on his interest.

"Cass," he breathed. His eyes were bright with relief and something that looked suspiciously like tenderness. "You're safe now, and help is on the way."

"But how did you—"

He put a finger to my lips. "My client, Dan, told my boss and me that he'd seen a blonde in a yellow trench coat being abducted at gunpoint on a sailboat. I knew it had to be you."

Okay, so in retrospect, yellow wasn't exactly an ideal color for spywear. But hey, it wasn't a Catwoman suit.

"Here comes the Coast Guard," a deep voice shouted.

I turned my head and saw the sailboat that Zac had been preparing to show anchored beside the rock with a tall, forty-something male aboard.

Zac caressed my cheek. "We're going to get you to the hospital to make sure you're all right."

"No. I'm fine." I tried to prop myself up on my elbows but was waylaid by a wave of dizziness.

He wrapped his powerful arms around me and eased me back onto his jacket. After smoothing my wet, tangled hair from my face, he kissed me—on the forehead.

I opened my mouth to tell him about the sun in my pocket, but I puked up another quart of water. And maybe a small fish.

Then everything went black again.

* * *

"Look who's awake," the matronly nurse said as she flung open the blinds.

The morning sun sliced into my eyes like a scalpel, so I pulled the covers over my head.

"How you feeling?" she asked.

Before I could tell her that my head hurt, I was starving, and I needed an IV of espresso, she threw back the blanket and stuck a thermometer under my tongue.

"Your concussion was mild," she explained as she adjusted a bobby pin in her gray, upswept hair, "so I'm sure the doctor will release you today. As soon as he gives me the go ahead, I'll start the paperwork."

She grabbed my wrist and fell silent as she took my pulse.

There was a knock at the door, and Detective Ohlsen entered with Detective Marshall in tow.

My heart rate sped up at the mere sight of them.

Detective Ohlsen approached the bed and snuck a sideways glance at the no-nonsense nurse. "How's the patient doing, Wanda?"

"Fine until you two walked in the room." She tossed my arm on the bed. "Then her blood pressure spiked."

Tattletale. I slid deeper into the sheets.

Detective Ohlsen bowed his head and clasped his hands behind his back. "Mind if we have a word with her?"

"I do, but it's visiting hours, so I don't have a say." She shook a patient file at him. "But don't you tire her out, Bud. You hear me?"

"Yes, ma'am."

She gave him the eagle eye and strode from the room.

"Nice manners," Detective Marshall—the king of courtesy—commented.

Detective Ohlsen and I shared a secret smile, and then he put his fist to his mouth and cleared his throat.

"After getting your note from Officer Stallone yesterday," he began with a stern stare, "I was on my way to arrest you. It was the only way I had to protect you from yourself. But then the call came in about an abduction down at the docks."

"I guess you're here to find out why it was me," I said, hoping to steer their thoughts away from the little matter of my impending arrest.

"Oh, we know," Detective Marshall said, sticking out his chest. "We spent most of the night interrogating Prudence and Clyde."

I bolted upright and searched Detective Ohlsen's face for confirmation. "They survived?"

He nodded. "The boat was in bad shape, but the Coast Guard found Clyde still tied up inside. They picked up Prudence a few minutes later clinging to a tree trunk."

I remembered the crash that had sent me flying. "I wonder if that's what knocked me off the boat."

Detective Ohlsen jutted out his lower lip. "Could be. The starboard side of the boat looked like it'd been hit by something pretty big around."

The memory of just how close I'd come to death made my mouth go dry. I reached for a bottle of water on the bedside table and caught sight of my arms. They were so covered with scratches and marks that they reminded me of Bertha's threat to make a skin quilt from Margaret. "Did Prudence tell you about Bertha Braun during the interrogation?"

"She did," Detective Ohlsen replied as he sunk into an armchair next to my bed. "But we already had our eye on her as a possible connection to the Viagra ring. She was Coveside Retirement Resort's most frequent visitor."

I might be a regular too if Santiago didn't live there.

Detective Marshall raised a clenched fist. "Now we finally have a witness who can testify to her involvement, so we can put her away where she belongs."

"Is Bertha in custody?" I asked in a hopeful tone.

He gave a self-satisfied smile. "We picked her up this morning."

Relief washed over me. Even though my skin was all battered and bruised, it was nice to know I'd be keeping it—at least until Bertha got out of prison. "I can't say I'm sorry to hear that. She had a score to settle with me."

"Bertha had a score to settle with a lot of people," Detective Ohlsen said. "And yet she never uttered a word about the adoption ring."

"Because her blackmail scheme would've come to light," I said wryly.

"I'm sure that's why." He rubbed his eyes. "She didn't know that Prudence was Dr. Windom's niece though. Apparently, he'd always referred to her as 'Rue.'"

That name was much more fitting, as far as I was concerned.

"However," he continued, "Bertha did say that your cousin told her Prudence was on leave from a hospital in LA. But when we'd talked to Prudence the day before, she said she was unemployed. We did a little digging and discovered that her last job was at a hospital in Jackson, and that's when I started to wonder if you might've been onto something with that syringe wrapper. Of course, it wasn't until I got your note that it all finally made sense."

I beamed like the morning sun. I'd done a pretty good job of sleuthing, apart from my near burial at sea, and I'd made good on my promise to Lucy. "Does this mean—"

"The charges have been dropped against Miss O'Connell," Detective Marshall interrupted in a bored tone.

Now I was full-on blazing, but I knew that there was still one more thing to make right. "What about the Bible?"

Detective Ohlsen scratched his head. "Oddly enough, Clyde was the one who asked the Coast Guard to retrieve that Bible from the boat. We'll be turning it over to the authorities in Jackson for follow-up."

I leaned back in bed, content. It looked like Clyde had a conscience, after all.

Wanda appeared in the doorway, and I was sorry to see that she wasn't holding a coffeepot or a food tray.

"The doctor is on his way." She put one hand on her hip and gestured toward the hallway with the other. "It's time for you two to scoot."

"Wanda's right, Lester," Detective Ohlsen said as he rose to his feet. "We need to let Miss Conti rest."

"Before you go, there's one last thing I need to know." I swallowed and picked at a thread hanging from the sheet. It was harder to pose the question than I'd imagined. "Did Prudence kill my uncle?"

Detective Ohlsen put his hands on his hips. "She says she didn't, and I believe her."

"Why?" I exclaimed. "She's a cold-blooded murderer."

"Well, for one thing," he began, "we haven't ruled out the possibility that your uncle's death was connected to the Viagra. And based on the phone activity his receptionist reported, we have reason to believe that he was involved in at least one other illicit activity that could have been a factor in his demise."

I gaped at him, dumbstruck. My family had been wrong about my uncle. He was no black sheep—he was a Tasmanian devil. "What else could he have possibly been doing?"

"That's classified." His face grew serious. "The other reason I think she's telling the truth is that she voluntarily confessed to smothering the doctor who'd delivered her, Jonas Thorpe, when he was hospitalized for a stroke."

I couldn't believe my ears. "But, the papers said he died from that stroke."

"That's what the medical examiner thought too," Detective Ohlsen said. "So, if she confessed to Dr. Thorpe's murder, then I feel confident that she would've admitted to killing your uncle if she'd done it."

"I agree," I whispered, still in shock.

Detective Ohlsen headed for the door. "We need to get back to the station now. Would you like for me to send an officer to escort you home?"

The mention of home seemed surreal, like I'd been away on a long journey. And then I realized something—besides the fact that Detective Ohlsen had basically just given me a "Get out of Jail Free" card—no one was here waiting for me.

"I've got the ride covered, Detective," Zac announced from the doorway.

I turned to look at him, and my stomach did a flip—in part because he was holding a to-go bag from The Apple Tree.

Zac winked and raised what looked like a double espresso from Carolyn's.

And I thought that he'd never looked more heroic.

* * *

"What's going on?" I asked as Zac turned onto Fletcher Way. The short street was lined with cars.

He slowed the Jeep to a crawl. "I don't know, but there's no place to park in front of the salon, and the parking lot looks full too."

"I'll bet Filly's having another fish fry," I said, getting steamed. "If he told his clients to use my lot again, I'm going to gut him and stuff him like a flounder."

Zac cast a concerned glance my way.

"Pull around back and park behind the Ferrari."

As he turned into the lot, I thought I saw an orange bodybuilder wearing eyeliner, a gold armband, and a wraparound skirt enter the back door.

I sat very still for a moment and then turned to Zac. "Did you see that?"

He turned off the ignition. "What?"

"Never mind." I rubbed my eyes and wondered whether it was normal to hallucinate from a concussion.

Zac hopped out of the car and opened my door.

As soon as my feet touched the ground, I heard Steve Martin's "King Tut" blaring on a stereo. My lips and fists curled. "I'll sacrifice her to the gods. That's what I'll do."

"Who?" Zac asked, looking alarmed.

I pushed past him and burst through the break room into the salon. And then I was knocked out—not literally, but figuratively. The Clip and Sip had been transformed into ancient Alexandria—Gia's version, that is. The walls were draped in shimmering gold fabric with pictures of pyramids and Egyptian symbols everywhere. There was even a mannequin wrapped like a mummy and a long cardboard box that had been painted like a sarcophagus.

Even more surprising, the salon was jam-packed. The lobby was standing room only, and all six of the salon chairs were filled. And the orange spray-tanned guy that I thought I'd hallucinated was going around fanning women with a Swiffer duster extender and feeding them grapes, figs, and cheese—from his hands.

Gia was the first to notice me. "Cass!" She engulfed me in a hug. "I'm so glad you're okay. I hope you don't mind that I didn't come to the hospital to pick you up. It's just that the response to the Queen of the Nile promotion has been so overwhelming."

"Are you kidding?" I exclaimed. "I'm thrilled."

"We're booked solid for the rest of the week, and the phone is ringing off the hook. I had to hire a temporary receptionist and stylists to fill the empty stations."

I threw my arms around her. "I'm so sorry I ever doubted you."

She blinked her blue-shadowed eyes. "You should be, *cug*. But don't apologize again, because it's just weird."

I laughed. "I just have one question. What's up with the Egyptian catsuit?"

"I'm Bastet, the cat goddess," she replied, touching her jeweled neck collar. "What else?"

The Bangles began to play, and a group of servants and harem girls began to "Walk Like an Egyptian" down the stairs. When they reached the dryers, they broke into the Jersey Turnpike. (Again, this was Gia's version of Egypt.)

I crossed my arms. "Where did you find these people?"

"They're Donatello's gym buddies. Luckily, they have a bodybuilding competition this weekend, so I didn't have to pay for their spray tans."

Someone tapped me on the back.

I turned to see Lucy dressed as Nefertiti, and we exchanged a long, silent embrace.

"Cass," she began, her eyes filling with tears, "how I can ever repay you?"

I smiled. "You can start by not crying. Seriously, though, you helped me by agreeing to work for me when no one else in town would. As far as I'm concerned, you saved me, and I saved you, and now we're even. So get back to your client and have some fun."

She grinned. "Whatever you say, Boss."

The front door of the salon opened, and four bodybuilders came in carrying a cot with Donna Bocca dressed as Cleopatra.

I should have been shocked, but I'd seen a lot of outrageous things since I'd started living with Gia. "Why's Donna getting the royal treatment?"

"You don't think I relied solely on my flyers to get the word out, do you?" Gia gave her signature hair-flip. "I promised her that she could be the queen of the party if she used her mighty mouth to spread the word around town."

"You know," I said, "if you put your mind to it, you could rule the world." And I was half-serious.

"I just want to rule the makeup world," she said, glancing at the clock. "Oh. I have to get my station ready for my twelve o'clock appointment with Amy. I offered her a discount on a makeover, and she thinks that just involves makeup. Little does she know that she's going to leave here with two distinct eyebrows."

"Good luck with that," I said, imagining the follicle fallout.

My message tone sounded, and I pulled out my phone. It was the results of my accounting exam. I was so excited about the success of the salon that school didn't matter at the moment. But I opened the e-mail anyway, and I almost fainted. I'd passed the class with a 72 on the exam, thanks to the curve.

I turned to find Zac to tell him my good news, but he was gone. I scanned the salon and spotted him in the lobby—with the bleached-blonde brigade! I started to stomp upstairs to my room, but then I reminded myself that this was the new, courageous Cassidi. I'd fought for my college degree, my salon, my friend, and even my life. Now I was going to have to fight for my guy too.

I took a deep breath and marched over to the four of them to tell them a thing or two.

"Cassidi," Zac began, holding up his hand as though to stop me, "I'd like to introduce you to my sisters, Grace, Helen, and Jackie."

Talk about taking the wind out of my sails. "It's such a pleasure to meet you," I said. And I meant it.

Grace squeezed my hand. "Zac talks about you all the time."

"Right?" Helen chimed in.

"Like, constantly," Jackie added.

"Thanks, you guys," he said, turning pink.

Sensing his discomfort, I decided to help him out despite the fact that he'd left me in the dark about his sisters. "Would you three excuse us for a moment? I need to talk to your brother outside."

"Of course," Grace said, and then she exchanged a knowing look with Helen and Jackie.

I pulled him by the hand onto the porch. "Why didn't you tell me they were your sisters?"

He opened his arms wide. "You never gave me the chance."

"I'm sorry about that." I put my head down. "I guess I was a little—"

"Jealous?" he interrupted as he tilted my chin up to his face.

I nodded, and he pulled me to his chest.

"Good," he breathed. His lips descended on mine, and I'm happy to report that this time he didn't blow.

When we came up for air, he looked me in the eyes. "You're a hero, Cass."

I twisted my mouth to one side. "I'm sure Duncan Pickles is having a field day with the story."

"It's not just local," Zac said. "The story went national. So now everyone knows how terrific you are."

"The only one I care about is you," I said softly.

He kissed me again, longer and deeper this time.

When he finally released me, I led him to the porch steps. I had a small item that was burning a hole in my pocket, and, well, my knees were weak. "I have something you'll be interested to see."

He shot me a sly smile. "Yes, you do."

"It's nothing like that," I exclaimed as I smacked him on the arm. I reached into the pocket of my jeans and pulled out an old silver coin. I handed it to Zac, and his eyes grew as wide as the antique currency.

"It's a Spanish peso," he said in an incredulous tone. "Where did you get this?"

"I found it wedged in a crack at the tip of Pirate's Hook."

He turned the coin over in his hands. "It had to come from Drake's treasure. His was the only ship that would've had them in this part of the country."

"I think Bart Coffyn must've hidden it there when he was put in the gibbet." I snuggled up close to him. "Did you see the scratch marks on the back? I think it's some kind of map."

"This is incredible." He turned and stared at me. "You're incredible."

I fluffed my hair.

"This means that my dad was right," he said, clenching the coin in his fist. "The treasure is here in Danger Cove."

"I think so too." I rubbed his thigh. "Wouldn't it be amazing if you bought his company back with the money from the treasure he wanted to find?"

"It would be a dream." He stared into the distance for a moment and then shook his head. "You know, Dan bought that boat I showed him. He was impressed with the way it handled in the storm. So why don't we go to The Lobster Pot tonight to celebrate?"

"Um," I hedged, "can we please go someplace that doesn't involve the ocean? Like Gino's Pizzeria, maybe?"

"Don't tell me that you're afraid of the water now," he said, pulling me close.

I laid my head on his shoulder. "Maybe a little."

"Well, you'd better get over that," he said, nuzzling my ear, "because we have a treasure to hunt."

"Oh don't worry." I looked up at him dead serious. "If precious jewels are involved, I'll recover real quick."

RECIPES

Fredericksburg Peach Praline Pie

As a Fredericksburg, Texas, native, Cassidi loves her local peaches. But her favorite southern pie is amazing with any peaches, as long as they're ripe. Note: If you want to "Italian this recipe up" a bit, add a splash of Amaretto to the pie filling. You won't be sorry you did.

Ingredients
1 unbaked piecrust (9-inch) or your favorite piecrust recipe
1 teaspoon all-purpose flour
⅓ cup all-purpose flour
¼ cup sugar
¼ teaspoon salt
¼ teaspoon ground nutmeg
½ cup light corn syrup
3 eggs
3 cups fresh peaches, chopped
¼ cup butter, melted
¼ cup brown sugar, firmly packed
2 tablespoons butter, softened
½ cup pecans, coarsely chopped

Directions
Sprinkle 1 teaspoon flour over piecrust.

Add 3 tablespoons flour, sugar, salt, nutmeg, corn syrup, and eggs to a mixing bowl. Beat at medium speed with an electric mixer for 1 minute.

Fold in peaches and ¼ cup melted butter. Pour the mixture into the piecrust.

Mix together the remaining flour and brown sugar in a mixing bowl.

Cut in 2 tablespoons butter using a pastry blender until the mixture resembles coarse crumbs. Stir in chopped pecans.

Sprinkle the crumb mixture evenly over the pie filling.

Bake at 375 degrees for 45-50 minutes or until center of pie is set. Cover crust edges with foil after 35 minutes to prevent over browning.

Creole Custa

Smugglers' Tavern bartender Hope Foster serves up some really cool drinks. For the Save the Lighthouse Committee fundraiser, she chose a chili-infused cocktail created in the spicy city of New Orleans in the mid-1800s.

Ingredients
1½ oz Demerara rum
¾ ounce fresh lemon juice
¼ oz chili flake-infused Clément Créole Shrubb orange liqueur
¼ oz turbinado sugar syrup (2 parts sugar, 1 part water)
2 dashes Dr. Adam Elmegirab's Dandelion & Burdock Bitters
Toasted benne seeds
Turbinado sugar

Directions
Mix the turbinado sugar and toasted benne seeds. Dampen the rim of a cocktail glass with lemon juice and then coat it with the sugar and seed mixture.

Add the remaining ingredients to a shaker and fill with ice. Shake and double strain the liquid into the rimmed cocktail glass.

Cleopatra's Asp

Gia concocted this coffee cocktail to keep The Clip and Sip clients caffeinated and lubricated during her Queen of the Nile promotion.

Ingredients
Turkish coffee
Grappa

Directions
Brew one pot (or one cup) of Turkish coffee. Douse liberally with grappa (at least one shot per cup). If this drink doesn't bite you in the asp, nothing will!

BOOK CLUB QUESTIONS

In *A Deadly Dye and a Soy Chai*, Cassidi is ashamed of the Victorian house that she inherited from her Uncle Vinnie because of its lurid past. Do you think she is right to feel this way?

Cassidi is also horrified by her late Uncle Vinnie's "art collection." Is there an object in your home or an heirloom in your family that embarrasses you? What is it?

If you could visit Danger Cove, where would you most like to go? And whom would you most want to meet?

Cassidi is addicted to espresso and Fredericksburg peaches, and Gia loves flavored vodka and Nutella. What's your favorite vice?

Gia and Amy enjoy Italian and German food. What's your favorite ethnic food? Do you have any ethnic recipes that have been handed down in your family? What are they?

Leona Hawthorne, a.k.a. Margaret Appleby, had interesting taste in reading. Have you read any of the books on her shelf? If not, what is the most controversial book you've ever read (besides *Fifty Shades of Grey*, of course)?

The color blue is prominent in *A Deadly Dye and a Soy Chai*. What does it represent for Prudence? And what does it mean to you?

Do you think Detective Ohlsen should have arrested Cassidi for interfering in the investigation? Why or why not?

Uncle Vinnie's death is still an unsolved mystery. Why do you think he was killed?

Most importantly, do you think Cassidi and Zac are a good match?

BOOKS BY TRACI ANDRIGHETTI

Danger Cove Mysteries
Deadly Dye & a Soy Chai
A Poison Manicure & Peach Liqueur
Killer Eyeshadow & a Cold Espresso

ABOUT THE AUTHORS

Traci Andrighetti is the *USA Today* bestselling author of the Danger Cove Hair Salon Mysteries as well as other works. In her previous life, she was an award-winning literary translator and a Lecturer of Italian at the University of Texas at Austin, where she earned a PhD in Applied Linguistics. But then she got wise and ditched that academic stuff for a life of crime—writing, that is.

To learn more about Traci, visit her online at:
www.traciandrighetti.com

Elizabeth Ashby was born and raised in Danger Cove and now uses her literary talent to tell stories about the town she knows and loves. Ms. Ashby has penned several Danger Cove Mysteries, which are published by Gemma Halliday Publishing. While she does admit to taking some poetic license in her storytelling, she loves to incorporate the real people and places of her hometown into her stories. She says anyone who visits Danger Cove is fair game for her poisoned pen, so tourists beware! When she's not writing, Ms. Ashby enjoys gardening, taking long walks along the Pacific coastline, and curling up with a hot cup of tea, her cat, Sherlock, and a thrilling novel. She is also purely fictional.

If you enjoyed this book, be sure to pick up the next Danger Cove Mystery:

KILLER CLUE AT THE OCEAN VIEW
Danger Cove Mysteries book #6

When Bree Milford's glamorous Big City career fails to materialize, she slinks home to the sleepy town of Danger Cove to reorganize and figure out her life. She agrees to run the family's Ocean View Bed & Breakfast while her parents go on vacation. Small town life becomes but dull when during a renovation a dead body falls out of the B&B's wall!

www.GemmaHallidayPublishing.com